# Ronicky Doone's Treasure

G·K
Hall
&Cº

Also published in Large Print
from G.K. Hall by Max Brand ™:


*Tiger Man*
*Ronicky Doone*
*Western Tommy*
*Smiling Charlie*
*The Rancher's Revenge*
*Tragedy Trail*
*Valley of Vanishing Men*
*Hunted Riders*
*The Bandit of the Black Hills*
*Silvertip's Roundup*
*The Nighthawk Trail*
*The Fastest Draw*
*The Stolen Stallion*
*Gun Gentleman*

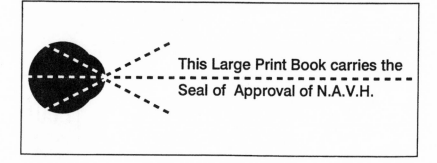

This Large Print Book carries the
Seal of Approval of N.A.V.H.

# Ronicky Doone's Treasure

## Max Brand ™

G.K. Hall & Co.
Thorndike, Maine

Published in 1994 by arrangement with Golden West Literary
Agency.

G.K. Hall Large Print Western Collection.

The text of this Large Print edition is unabridged.
Other aspects of the book may vary from the original edition.

Set in 16 pt. News Plantin by Warren Doersam.

Printed in the United States on acid-free paper.

**Library of Congress Cataloging in Publication Data**

Brand, Max, 1892–1944.
   Ronicky Doone's treasure / Max Brand.
     p.    cm.
   ISBN 0-8161-5998-X (alk. paper : lg. print)
   1. Large type books.  I. Title.
  [PS3511.A87R67  1994]
  813'.52—dc20                        94-13482

# CONTENTS

# CHAPTER I

# STRANGE COMPANY

Snow had already fallen above timber line, and the horseman, struggling over the summit, looked eagerly down into the broad valleys below, dark with evergreens. There was half an hour more of sunshine, but by the time he had ridden through the belt of lodge-pole pines, those stubborn marchers up to the mountaintops, a stiffening north wind had sheeted the sky from horizon to horizon with clouds.

Even before the rain began he put on his slicker to turn the edge of the gale, but, as he came out of the pines and into the more open and gently rolling lands beyond, the rain was beginning to drive down the valley. The lower he dropped toward the bottom lands the lower dropped the storm clouds above him, until the summits were quite lost in rolling gray masses and a mist of thin rain slanted across the trail.

The mare turned her head sideways to it, taking the brunt on one flattened ear and from time to time shaking off the drops of moisture. Between her and the rider there existed an almost conversational intimacy, it seemed. He had spread out

7

the skirt of his slicker so as to cover as great a portion of her barrel as possible; as the chill of the rain increased, he encouraged her with talk. She replied with a slight pricking of her ears from time to time and often threw up her head in that way horses have when they wish to see the master the more clearly.

Meanwhile, she descended the precipitous trail with such cat-footed activity that it was plain she had spent her life among the mountains. The rider made little effort to direct her but allowed her to follow her own fancy, as though confident that she would take the quickest way to the bottom of the slope. This, indeed, she did, sometimes slackening her pace for a moment to study the lay of the land ahead, sometimes taking a steep down pitch on braced legs, sometimes wandering in easy loops to one side or the other.

In such a manner she came in the dusk of that late, stormy afternoon to the almost level going of the valley floor. Now it was possible to see her at her best, for she sprang out in a smooth and stretching gallop with such easily working muscles that her gait was deceptively fast. Here, again, the rider simply pointed out the goal and then let her take her own way toward it.

That goal was the only building in sight. Perhaps for miles and miles it was the only structure, and the face of the rider brightened as he made out the sharp angle of the roof. The ears of the mare pricked. Their way across the mountains had been a long one; they had been several hours in the snows above timber line; and this promise of shelter was a golden one.

But it was a deceptive promise, for when they came in the face of the driving storm they found that the tall building was not a ranch house but merely a ruined barn. It had once been a portion of a large establishment of some cattle owner, but the house proper and its outlying structures had melted away with the passage of time and the beating of such storms as that of this day. The sheds were mere crumbling ridges; the house was a ragged mound from which rotting timber ends projected. Only the barn subsisted.

It was of vast size. Hundreds of tons of loose hay could have been stored in its mow; scores of horses could have been stalled along its sides. And it had been built with such unusual solidity that, whereas the rest of the buildings had disintegrated, this one kept its original dimensions intact through half of its length. The south front was whole. Only the northern portion of the building had crushed in. But for some reason this combination of ruin and repair was more melancholy than the utter destruction of the rest of the ranch.

The horseman regarded this sight with a shake of the head and then looked again up the valley. But it would be difficult to continue. By this time it must have been sunset, and the storm dimmed the earth to the colors of late twilight. Every moment the wind freshened out of the north, picking up the drifts of rain and whirling them into gray ghost forms. To continue down a blind trail in

9

the face of this gale, with no definite destination, was madness. The horseman resigned himself with a sigh to staying in the ruined barn until dawn.

He rode the mare, therefore, through a fallen section of the south front of the structure and into what had once been the mow. Stale scents of moldy straw still lingered in it.

Once inside, there was barely sufficient light to show the wanderer the dim outlines of the barn, and it was even more imposing in dimensions from within than from without. To the roof was a dizzy rise. A broad space extended on either side to the supporting walls. Half a regiment might bivouac here. Most important of all, the north gable was almost entirely blocked. That end of the building, though fallen, had not yet crumbled to the ground, and the broken roof formed a sort of enormous apron extending against the wind.

As soon as he had discovered this, the wanderer began at once to make systematic preparations for spending the night. He first rode the mare back into the open air to a rain rivulet, where she was allowed to drink. Then he returned, dismounted, gathered some fragments of wood, and lighted a fire.

The first leap of the yellow light transfigured the gloomy place. It started a shudder and dance of great shadows among the network of rafters above and in the corners of the building; it also showed the mare, from which the traveler now removed the saddle and rubbed her down — a bit of work of which most of the other riders of the Rocky Mountains would not have thought. He dried her as well as he could, and, before paying the slightest attention to his own wants, he produced from his saddle bags a mixture of chopped hay and crushed barley, a provision for his horse which he carried with him wherever he went. His glance wandered affectionately over her, for truly she was a beautiful creature.

In color she was a rich bay. Her stature was rather less than the average, for she was not more than fifteen hands and three inches in height; but what she lacked in height she made up in the exquisite nicety of her proportions. At first glance she looked rather too fine for hard mountain work, but a little closer examination showed ample girth at the cinches, nobly sloped shoulders, and quarters to match. In fact, she could have carried a heavy-weight, and the bulk of her owner was a trifle for her strength.

He proved a slenderly made fellow as he turned away from the mare and threw more wood on the fire — a man of medium height and in no way imposing physically. His carriage alone struck the eye. He was erect as a whipstock, bore his head high and proudly, and moved with a light, quick step, as though he had been forced to act quickly so often that the habit had formed and hardened on him. That alert and jaunty carriage would in itself have won him some respect, even if his name had not been Ronicky Doone, whose fame in the more southerly ranges was already a notable thing. Horse-breaker, mischief-maker, adventurer by in-

11

stinct, and fighter for sheer love of battle, he carried on his young body enough scars to have decked out half a dozen hardy warriors of the mountains, but the scars were all he had gained. The quarrels he fought had been the quarrels of others; and, a champion of lost causes, the rewards of his actions went to others.

Now he rolled down his blanket beside the fire, which he had built for the sake of warmth and good cheer rather than for cooking. His fare consisted of hard crackers and was finished off with a draft of cold water from his canteen; then he was ready for sleep.

He found shelter at the north end of the mow. Here a great section of the disintegrating roof had fallen and stood end up, walling away a little room half a dozen paces in length and something more than half of that in width. By the vague light cast from the fire, which was rapidly blackening under the downpour of the rain, he took up his new abode for the night, and Lou followed him into it, unbidden.

He was wakened, after how long an interval he could not guess, by the sound of Lou getting to her feet, and a moment later he heard voices sounding in the big mow of the barn. Other travelers had taken refuge from the storm, it seemed. Ronicky Doone, glad of a chance to exchange words with men, rose hastily and walked to the entrance to his quarters.

As he did so, a match was lighted, revealing two men standing beside their horses in the center

12

of the great inclosure.

"A fine place for a meeting," said he who held the match. "How come we got to ride out here to the end of the world?"

His companion answered: "Maybe you'd have us meet up in a hotel or something, where the sheriff could scoop the whole bunch of us in. Is that your idea, Marty?"

Ronicky Doone had already advanced a step toward the newcomers, but as he heard these speeches he slipped back again, and, putting his hand over the nose of Lou, he hissed a caution into her ear. And glad he was that he had taught her this signal for silence. She remained at his back, not daring to stir or make a sound, and Ronicky, with a beating heart, crouched behind his barrier to spy on these strangers.

# CHAPTER II

## THE PLOT

"All I say, 'Baldy' McNair," said Marty, "is that the old man is sure stepping out long and hard to make things seem as mysterious as he can. Which they ain't no real need to come clean out here. This makes fifty miles I've rode, and you've come nigher onto eighty. What sense is in that, Baldy?"

The match burned out. Baldy spoke in the dark.

"Maybe the work he's got planned out lies ahead — lies north."

"Maybe. But it sure grinds in on me the way he works. Never no reasons. Just orders. 'Meet here to-day after sunset.' That's all he says. I up and asks him: 'Why after sunset, Jack? Afraid they'll be somebody to see us out there — a coyote or something, maybe?' But he wouldn't answer me nothing. 'You do what I say,' says he, 'and figure out your reasons for yourself.' That's the way he talks. I say: Is it fit and proper to talk to a gent like he was a slave?"

"Let's start a fire," said his companion. "Talk a pile better when we get some light on the subject."

In a minute or two they had collected a great pile of dry stuff; a little later the flames were leaping up in great bodies toward the roof and puffing out into the darkness.

The firelight showed Ronicky two men who had thrown their dripping slickers back from their shoulders. Marty was a scowling fellow with a black leather patch over his right eye. His companion justified his nickname by taking off his hat and revealing a head entirely and astonishingly free from hair. From the nape of his neck to his eyebrows there was not a vestige or a haze of hair. It gave him a look strangely infantile, which was increased by cheeks as rosy as autumn apples.

"Now," went on Baldy McNair, "let me put something in your ear, Lang. A lot of the boys have heard you knock the chief. Which maybe the chief himself has heard."

"He's give no sign," muttered Marty.

"Son," said Baldy, who was obviously much younger than the man of the patched eye, but who apparently gained dignity by the baldness of his head, "when Jack Moon gives a sign, it's the first sign and the last sign all rolled into one. First you'll hear of it will be Moon asking you to step out and talk to him. And Moon'll come back from that talk alone and say that you started out sudden on a long trip. You wouldn't be the first. There was my old pal 'Lefty' and 'Gunner' Matthews. There was more, besides. Always that way! If they start getting sore at the way he runs things, he just takes them out walking, and they all go on that long journey that you'll be taking one of these days if you don't mind your talk, son! I'm telling you because I'm your friend, and you can lay to that!"

"What I don't see," answered Marty Lang, "is why the chief wants to hang onto a gent forever. You make it out? Once in the band, always in the band. That ain't no sense. A gent don't want to stick to this game forever."

"Oh, ho!" chuckled Baldy. "Is that the way of it? Well, son, don't ever let the chief hear you say that! Sure we get tired of having to ride wherever he tells us to ride, and we want to settle down now and then — or we think that we want to — and lead a quiet life and have a wife and a house and a family and all that. For that matter, there's nothing to keep us from it. The chief don't object."

"Don't object? How can a gent settle down at any thing when he's apt to get a call from the chief any minute?"

"Wrong again. Not more'n once every six months. That's about the average. And then it's always something worth while. How long you been with us?"

"Four years."

"Ever gone hungry for four years?"

"No."

"When you was sick, two years back, were you took care of?"

"Sure."

"What did you have when the chief picked you up?"

"Nothing."

16

"All right. You were down to zero. He picked you up. He gave you a chance to live on the fat. All you got to do in return is to ride with him once in six months and to promise never to leave the band. Why? Because he knows that if ever a gent shakes clear of it he'll be tempted to start talking some day, and a mighty little talk would settle the hash of all of us. That's the why of it! He's a genius, Moon is. How long d'you think most long riders last?"

"I dunno. They get bumped off before long."

"Sure they do. Know why? Because the leaders have always kept their men together in a bunch most of the time. Moon seen that. What does he do? He gets a picked lot together. He gets a big money scheme all planned. Then he calls in his men. Some of 'em come fifty miles. Some of 'em live a hundred miles away. They all come. They make a dash and do the work. Soon's it's done they scatter again. And the posse that takes the tracks has five or six different trails to follow instead of one. Result? They get all tangled up. Jack Moon has been working twenty years and never been caught once! And he'll work twenty years more, son, and never be caught. Because why? Because he's a genius! Steady up! Who's that?"

Straight through the entrance to the mow came two riders.

"Silas Treat and the chief himself," said Lang.

What Ronicky Doone saw were two formidable fellows. One, mounted on a great roan horse, was a broad-shouldered man with a square-cut black beard which rolled halfway down his chest. The other was well-nigh as large, and when he came into the inner circle of the firelight Ronicky saw one of those handsome, passionless faces which never reveal the passage of years. Jack Moon, according to Baldy, had been a leader in crime for twenty years, and according to that estimate he must be at least forty years old; but a casual glance would have placed him closer to thirty-three or four. He and his companion now reined their horses beside the fire and raised their hands in silent greeting. The black-bearded man did not speak. The leader, however, said:

"Who started that fire?"

"My idea," confessed Baldy. "Matter of fact, we both had the same idea. Didn't seem anything wrong about starting a fire and getting warm and dry."

"I seen that fire a mile away," said the leader gloomily. "It was a fool idea."

"But they's nobody else within miles."

"Ain't there? Have you searched all through the barn?"

"Why — no."

"How d'you know somebody didn't come here?"

"But who'd be apt to come this way?"

"Look at those cinders over there. That shows that somebody lately has been here and started a fire. If they come here once, why not again?"

"I didn't notice that place," said Baldy regretfully. "Sure looks like I've been careless. But I'll

18

give the barn a search now."

"Only one place to look," said Jack Moon, "and that's behind that chunk of the roof where it's fallen down yonder."

"All right!" The other nodded and started straight for the hiding place of Ronicky Doone.

The latter reached behind him and patted the nose of the mare, Lou, in sign that she must still preserve the utmost silence. Then he drew his revolver. There was no question about what would happen if he were discovered. He had been in a position to overhear too many incriminating things. Unlucky Baldy, to be sure, would be an easy prey. But the other three? Three to one were large odds in any case, and every one of these men was formidable.

Straight to the opening came Baldy and peered in, though he remained at a distance of five or six paces. Ronicky Doone poised his gun, delayed the shot, and then frowned in wonder. Baldy had turned and was sauntering slowly back toward his companions.

"Nothing there," he said to the chief, as he approached.

Ronicky hardly believed his ears, but a moment of thought explained the mystery. It was pitch dark behind that screening wall, and the darkness was rendered doubly thick by Baldy's probable conviction that there must be nothing to see behind the fallen roof section. He had come there prepared to find nothing, and he had found the sum of his expectations and no more.

"Sure there ain't?" and Jack Moon nodded. "Which don't mean that you wasn't a fool to light a fire and give somebody a light to shoot you by in case they was somebody lying around. Now, into the saddle both of you. We got a hard ride ahead."

"Something big on hand?" asked Marty Lang.

"There's a lesson for yaller-livered sneaks on hand," said Jack Moon, his deep bass voice floating smoothly back to the ear of Ronicky. "Hugh Dawn has come back to Trainor. We're going to drop in and call on him and ask him what he's been doing all these ten years."

The low, growling murmur of the other three rolled away in the rush of rain beyond the door of the barn. The four horsemen disappeared, and Ronicky stepped out into the light of the dying fire. He had hardly taken a step forward when he shrank back again against the wall.

Straight into the door came Jack Moon and peered uneasily about the barn. Then he whirled his horse away and disappeared into the thick downpour. He had seen nothing, and yet the true and suspicious instinct of the man had brought him back to take a final glance into the barn to make sure that no one had spied on the gathering of his little band.

# CHAPTER III

# THE DAWN HOUSE

Small things are often more suggestive, more illuminating, than large events. All that Ronicky had heard Baldy say about Jack Moon and his twenty years' career of crime had not been so impressive as that sudden reappearance of the leader with all the implications of his hair-trigger sensitiveness. Ronicky Doone was by no means a foolish dreamer apt to be frightened away from danger by the mere face of it, but now he paused.

Plainly Hugh Dawn was a former member of the band, and this trip of Moon was undertaken for the purpose, perhaps the sole purpose, of killing the offender who had left his ranks. Ronicky Doone considered. If Hugh Dawn had belonged to this crew ten years before, he had probably committed crimes as terrible as any in the band. If so, sympathy was wasted on him, for never in his life had Ronicky seen such an aggregation of dangerous men. It scarcely needed the conversation of Lang and Baldy to reveal the nature of the organization. Should he waste time and labor in attempting to warn Hugh Dawn of the coming trouble?

21

Trainor, he knew, was a little crossroads village some twenty miles to the north. He might outdistance the criminal band and reach the town before them, but was it wise to intervene between such a man as Jack Moon and his destined victim? Distinctly it was not wise. It might call down the danger on his own head without saving Dawn. Moreover, it was a case of thief against thief, murderer against murderer, no doubt. If Dawn were put out of the way, probably no more would be done than was just.

And still, knowing that the four bloodhounds were on the trail of one unwarned man, the spirit of Ronicky leaped with eagerness to be up and doing. Judgment was one thing, impulse was another, and all his life Ronicky Doone had been the creature of impulse. One man was in danger of four. All his love of fair play spurred him on to action.

In a moment more the saddle was on the back of the mare, he had swung up into his place, flung the slicker over his shoulders, and cantered through the door of the barn.

He turned well east of the trail which wound along the center of the valley. This, beyond question, the band would follow, but inside of half an hour Ronicky estimated that his mount, refreshed by her food and rest, would outfoot them sufficiently to make it safe to drop back into the better road without being in danger of meeting the four.

Such, accordingly, was the plan he adopted. He struck out a long semicircle of half a dozen miles, which carried him down into the central trail again; then he headed straight north toward Trainor. The rain had fallen off to a mere misting by this time, and the wind was milder and came out of the dead west, so that there was nothing to impede their progress. The mountains began to lift gloomily into view, the walls of the valley drew steadily nearer on either side, and at length, at the head of the valley, he rode into the town of Trainor.

With the houses dripping and the street a river of mud under the hoofs of Lou, the town looked like a perfect stage for a murder. Ronicky Doone dismounted in front of the hotel.

There was no one in the narrow hallway which served as clerk's office and lobby. He beat with the butt of his gun against the wall and shouted, for there was no time to delay. At the most he could not have outdistanced Jack Moon by more than half an hour, and that was a meager margin in which to reach the victim, warn him, and see him started in his flight.

Presently an old fellow with a goat beard stumbled down the stairs, rubbing his eyes.

"And what might you want this late, partner?" he inquired.

"Hugh Dawn," said Ronicky. "Where does Hugh Dawn live?"

"Hugh Dawn?" said the other, his eyes blank with the effort of thought. Then he shook his head. "Dunno as I ever heard about any Hugh Dawn. Might be you got to the wrong town, son."

It was partly disappointment, partly relief that

made Ronicky Doone sigh. After all, he had done his best; and, since his best was not good enough, Hugh Dawn must even die. However, he would still try.

"You're sure there's no Dawn family living in these parts?"

"Dawn family? Sure there is. But there ain't no Hugh Dawn ever I heard of."

"How long you been around here?"

"Eight years come next May Day."

"Very well," said Ronicky brusquely, recalling that it was ten years before that Hugh Dawn, according to Jack Moon, had disappeared. "Where is the Dawn house?"

"Old Grandpa Dawn," said the proprietor, "used to live out there, but he died a couple of years back. Now they ain't nobody but Jerry Dawn."

"The son?"

"It ain't a son. She's a girl. Geraldine is her name. Most always she's called Jerry, though. She teaches the school and makes out pretty good and lives in that big house all by herself."

"And where's the house, man?" cried Ronicky, wild with impatience.

"Out the east road about a couple of miles. Can't help knowing it, it's so big. Stands in the middle of a bunch of pines and —"

The rest of his words trailed away into silence. Ronicky Doone had whipped out of the door and down the steps. Once in the saddle of Lou again, he sent her headlong down the east road. Would he be too late, after this delay at the hotel and the talk with the dim-minded old hotel proprietor?

The house, as he had been told, was unmistakable. Dense foresting of pines swept up to it on a knoll well back from the road, and over the tops of the trees, through the misting rain and the night, he made out the dim triangle of the roof of the building. In a moment the hoofs of the mare were scattering the gravel of the winding road which twisted among the trees, and presently he drew up before the house.

The face of it, as was to be expected at this hour of the night, was utterly blank, utterly black. Only the windows, here and there, glimmered faintly with whatever light they reflected from the stormy night, the panes having been polished by the rain water. As he had expected, it was built in the fashion of thirty or forty years before. There were little decorative turrets at the four corners of the structure and another and larger turret springing from the center of the room. He had no doubt that daylight would reveal much carved work of the gingerbread variety.

A huge and gloomy place it was for one girl to occupy! He sprang from the saddle and ran up the steps and knocked heavily on the front door. Inside, he heard the long echo wander faintly down the hall and then up the stairs, like a ghost with swiftly lightening footfall. There was no other reply. So he knocked again, more heavily, and, trying the knob of the door, he found it locked fast. When he shook it there was the rattle of a chain on the inside. The door had been securely fastened, to be sure. This was not the rule in this country of wide-doored hospitality.

Presently there was the sound of a window being opened in the story of the house just above him. He looked up, but he could not locate it, since no lamp had been lighted inside.

"Who's there?" called a girl's voice.

It thrilled Ronicky Doone. He had come so far to warn a man that his life was in danger. He was met by this calm voice of a girl.

"Who I am doesn't matter," said Ronicky Doone. "I've come to find Hugh Dawn. Is he here?"

There was a slight pause, a very slight pause, and one which might have been interpreted as meaning any of a dozen things. Then: "No, Hugh Dawn is not here."

"Lady," said Ronicky Doone, "are you Geraldine Dawn?"

"Yes," said the voice. "I am she."

"I've heard of you," said Ronicky; "and I've heard of Hugh Dawn. I know that he's in this house. What I want to do is —"

"Whatever you want to do," broke in that amazingly mild voice, "you will have to wait till morning. I am alone in this house. I do not intend to have it entered before daylight comes. Hugh Dawn is not here. If you know anything about him, you also know that he hasn't been here for ten years."

And there was the sound of a window being closed with violence.

To persist in efforts at persuasion in the face of such a calm determination was perfect folly. Besides, there were many explanations. Perhaps Jack Moon had heard simply that Hugh Dawn was coming back to his home, and the traitor to the band had not yet arrived at his destination. Perhaps at that moment the leader was heading straight for a distant point on the road to lay an ambush. "Dawn is in Trainor," he had said, but that might be a metaphorical statement. It might simply mean that he was on the way toward the town. Or perhaps the fugitive had received a warning and had already fled. At any rate, Ronicky Doone felt that he had done more than enough to free his conscience.

But there was one thing that upset this conviction as Ronicky swung back into his saddle and turned the head of weary Lou back down the road through the pines. This was the memory of the voice of the girl. There is no index of character so perfect and suggestive as the voice, and that of Jerry Dawn was soft, quiet, steady. It had neither trembled with fear nor shrilled with indignation. If any of the blood of Hugh Dawn ran in her veins, then surely the man could not be altogether bad.

Of course, this was wild guesswork at best, but it carried a conviction to Ronicky, and when, halfway down to the main road, he remembered how Jack Moon had returned to the door of the barn to investigate a suspicion which was based on nothing but the most shadowy material — when, above all, he recalled how justified that suspicion was — Ronicky Doone determined to imitate the maneuver. For were there not reasons why the girl should refuse to admit that this man Hugh Dawn — her father, perhaps — had returned to his house?

No sooner had the determination come to Doone than he turned the head of his horse and swerved back toward the house for a second time. He now rode off the noisy gravel, walking Lou in the silent mold beneath the trees; and so he came back again to the edge of the clearing. Here he tethered the mare, skirted under shelter of the trees halfway around the house, and then ran swiftly out of the forest and up to the steep shelter of the wall of the dwelling. Here he paused to take breath and consider again what he had done and the possibilities that lay before him.

He could have laughed at the absurdity of what he had done. He was, in reality, stalking a big house which contained no more than one poor girl, badly frightened already, no doubt, in spite of that steady and brave voice. What he was actually doing was spying on the possibility of Hugh Dawn — trying to force himself on the man in order to save his life!

Very well. He would be a sane and thinking man once more. The devil might now fly away with Hugh Dawn for all of him. Let there be an end of this foolishness. Ronicky Doone would turn his back on Dawn and all connected with him. His own path led otherwhere.

28

He had made up his mind to this point and was turning away, when he heard that within the house which made him stop short and flatten his ear against the wall.

It has already been said that sound and echoes traveled easily in that frame building, with its time-dried wood. And now what Ronicky Doone heard was a slow repetition of creaking sounds one after another, moving through the second story of the building. He recognized the intervals; he recognized the nature of the squeaking and straining. Some very heavy person was moving by stealth, slowly, down one of the upper halls.

Certainly it was not the girl who had spoken to him. Could it be Hugh Dawn? Or was it a member of Moon's band, who might have slipped into the building from the rear, say?

Ronicky Doone intended to investigate.

# CHAPTER IV

## WARNING

He began at once to search for a means of entrance. Ordinarily he would have attempted to get in through one of the windows of the basement, but when he tried them, he found every one stanchly secured from within, and when he attempted to turn the catch with the blade of his knife, he could not succeed. The locks had been rusted strongly in place.

Since he could not take the bottom way in, he would take an upper. Yonder, the turret which projected from the upper corner of the building was continued all the way to the ground through the three stories of the house in a set of bow windows. The result was that between the angle of the projecting windows and the wall of the house itself there were scores of footholds, precarious and small to an inexpert climber, but to athletic Ronicky Doone as safe as walking up a stairway.

The chance to use his muscles, moreover, after this chilling wait, was welcome to him, and he went up with the agility of a monkey until he reached the smaller window on the third story of the structure. Here he clambered onto the pro-

30

jecting sill and tried to lift the window. It was locked as securely as those of the basement. There was only the chance that it might have been used more recently and had not been rusted into place.

Accordingly, he opened his stout-bladed knife again and inserted it in the crack between the upper and the lower sash, feeling along toward the center until he reached the little metal crossbar which made the windows secure. It resisted the first tentative pressure. But the second and more vigorous effort made the lock give with a faint squeaking sound. In another instant Ronicky had raised the window and thrust his head into the room.

His whole body followed at once, and, lowering himself cautiously into the room, he found himself at last definitely consigned to the adventure, whatever it might bring forth.

A new atmosphere had at once surrounded him. The air was warmer, less fresh, drier. But more than all these things, it was filled with the personality, so to speak, of human beings. The darkness had a quality not unlike that of a human face. It watched Ronicky Doone; it listened to him as he crouched by the wall and waited and listened.

For now, no matter how innocent his errand, the people of the house, if indeed there were more than the girl present, would be amply justified in treating as a criminal a man who had forced his way into their home. If he were shot on sight the law would not by the weight of a single finger attempt to punish the slayers. And still he per-

31

sisted in the adventure.

Eventually, by whatever uneasy light filtered from the night and through the window, he made out that the room in which he stood was utterly bare of furniture of any kind. It was deserted. By the soft feel of dust beneath his shoe he shrewdly guessed that it had been deserted a matter of many years, and when he tried the boards with his weight his conjecture was further reinforced by the whisper which replied, and which would have grown into a prodigious squeak had he allowed his whole weight to fall.

This particular made his exit from the room a delicate matter. He managed it without noise only by staying close to the edge of the wall, where the flooring, being here firmly attached, could not possibly have any great play. Facing out to the center of the room, since in this manner he could slide closest to the wall, he managed to get to the hall door of the room and thence into the hall without making a whisper loud enough to have caught the attentive ear of a cat.

Once there he paused again, swaying a little, so lightly was he poised, with the rhythm of his breathing. The house below was still as the grave, but presently it was filled with murmurs. For the wind had freshened and was now striking the house with a renewed vigor. His thought flashed back to Lou, standing patiently in the shelter of the pines, and then he turned again to the work before him.

It was peculiarly embarrassing. He could not

simply stand in the hall and shout his good intentions and his warnings. That would be sheer madness. There remained nothing but to hunt through the house and hope to find Hugh Dawn, surprise him, perhaps cover him with a gun, and then deliver his tidings at its point. For otherwise Hugh Dawn, no doubt in terrible fear of his old band, would shoot the first stranger on sight.

Ronicky began to slip down the hall. The noise of the wind, starting a thousand creaks in the house, favored his progress immensely. It covered other footfalls, to be sure, but it also covered his own. In order that the noise he made might be completely blanketed by the shakings of the wind, he waited for flurries of the storm and took advantage of them to make swift progress forward, then paused through the intervals of comparative silence.

So he fumbled down the upper hall balustrade until it swerved to the right and down, leading him onto the stairs. In this way he came down to the second story, where, he was sure, he had first heard the footfalls. It was in utter darkness. Yet by striving continually to pierce the wall of shadow he had so far accustomed his eyes to the strain that he could make out the vague proportions of that wide and lofty hall.

Where the stairs turned easily onto the hall flooring he paused a moment, in a lull of the gale, to wait for the next flurry and the crashing of the rain against the roof. The moment it began he started once more, turning to the right, determined to try each door he came to and so start a gradual examination of the house. But he had hardly taken a step on his way when a light click sounded close behind him, and then a shaft of light struck past his head.

Ronicky Doone whirled and dived down, not away from the direction of the light, but toward it, whipping out his revolver as he fell upon his supporting left arm. The shaft of light, launched from a pocket electric torch, was wandering wildly. Behind it he caught the dimly outlined figure of a man. Then the light fell on him as he gathered himself for another leap, and a revolver roared straight before him.

There was a twitch at the shoulder of his coat — the bullet had come as close as that! — then Ronicky Doone sprang, animallike, from hands to knees, swerving out of the flash of the light as the gun spoke again and missed again. He struck with his left hand as he shot in. All his force, multiplied threefold by nervous ecstasy, went into that whipping punch, and the knuckles crunched home against bone. It was a solid impact. The jar of it left his arm numb to the shoulder, and the vague outline of the man behind the light collapsed.

As he did so, the electric torch fell from his hand, spinning and filling the hall with wild flashings until it struck the floor. The revolver crashed to the boards an instant later, and Ronicky, scooping up the light, turned it down into the face of his victim.

It was a big body, lying with the long arms

thrown out crosswise, so completely stunning had the blow been. Ronicky, estimating the power in that now inert bulk, was grateful that his first punch had struck home. In a struggle hand to hand he would not have had a chance for victory.

Somewhere in the distance there was a woman's shrill cry of terror. Ronicky paid little heed to it, for he was too busy examining that upturned face. His victim was a man of about forty-five, with a seamed and lined face, clean shaven, rather handsome, and sadly worn by the passage of time and many troubles, no doubt. But the expression was neither savage nor sneaking. The forehead was broad and high with noble capacity for thought. The nose was strongly but not cruelly arched. The mouth was sensitive. If this were Hugh Dawn, he was by no means the criminal type as Ronicky Doone knew it, and in his wanderings he had known many a yegg, many a robber.

The knocked-out man began to revive and came suddenly to his senses, sitting up and blinking at the dazzling shaft of light. Then he reached for his fallen gun, but the foot of Ronicky stamped over it at the same instant.

All this, of course, from the first snapping on of the light, had filled only a few seconds. Now the calling of the girl broke out clearly upon them as she threw open a door. Ronicky saw her form rushing down toward them and heard the rustling of her clothes. There was the dim flicker of a gun in her hand.

"Lady," said Ronicky, holding the electric light far from him, but still keeping it focused on the face of the other man so that his own body would be in deep comparative shadow. "I'm here for no harm. But mind your gun. If this is Hugh Dawn — if he means anything to you — mind what you do. I've got him covered!"

"Oh, dad!" cried the girl excitedly. "Are you —"

"I'm not hurt," replied the other. "They've got me, that's all. Stand up?"

"Stand up," said Ronicky. "Are you Hugh Dawn?"

The other rose. He was even larger than he had seemed when he was lying on the floor, and his glance wistfully sought his fallen revolver.

"I'm Hugh Dawn, right enough," he said. "I don't figure that you knew that?" And he sneered mockingly at Ronicky. The girl, despite the warnings of Ronicky, had slipped to his side. Now he caught the revolver out of her hand and glared at his captor.

"I see the gun," said Ronicky. "Don't try any play with it, Mr. Dawn. I'm sure watching you close. Understand?"

The other nodded and swallowed. But there was a desperate determination about his face that made Ronicky uneasy.

"Where's — the chief?" gasped Hugh Dawn. "Where's he?"

36

And his glance rolled up and down the hall.

"Not here," said Ronicky, "but coming."

The other quaked and then shrugged his shoulders.

"Well?"

"Get me straight," said Ronicky. "I've not come here to get you. If I wanted to do that I could shoot you down now. I want something else."

"I know what you want," shouted the other, "but you won't get it! Not if I have to die ten times! Never!"

"What you're talking about," said Ronicky, "I don't know. Here's my yarn; believe it or not, as you want to! I lay out in a barn to-night, heard Jack Moon and his crew plot to come here and grab you, and rode on around them to give you a warning. That's why I'm here. I tried to get through the door. The lady, here, wouldn't talk to me. I played a hunch that you might be here, anyway. I came back, shinnied up the wall, opened a window, and here I am. Does that sound like straight talk to you?"

"Straight enough," said the other gloomily. "Except that it's a lie. Moon and you and the rest — I know I'm through with my trail. I know that I got my back agin' the wall, but I don't care a rap for you all! I won't beg, and I won't tell you where Purchass hid his stuff. That's final! Bring on Moon. I'll tell him the same thing!"

# CHAPTER V

# HIS HAT IN THE RING

What it all meant Ronicky could only vaguely guess. It was not only the death of Dawn that Moon wished. The renegade also possessed a secret which the outlaws considered beyond price, and for the retention of this secret the man was willing to lay down his life. Naturally enough, the man refused to believe that Ronicky was not an agent of the leader.

"Partner," said Ronicky, "my name's Doone. I ain't very well known up around these parts of the range, but down farther south they'll tell you that I'm a tolerable square shooter. Maybe I ain't any wonder, but nobody that walks on two feet ever accused me of lying. And I give you my word of honor that I got nothing to do with Jack Moon or whatever his name is — him and his men. I've come here to tell you the straight of what I heard tonight. I rode ahead to warn you to start on your way if you want to start without being salted down with lead."

The other was staggered a little.

"How come you to beat out Moon?" he asked.

"I've got the fastest trick in the line of hossflesh

that ever packed a saddle," said Ronicky proudly. "I got half an hour to the good on Moon. But you've used up most of that time already. I say, Dawn, if you want to save your life and your secret, whatever that is, start riding now!"

"And jump into the hands of Moon the minute I leave the house?" cried Dawn, the perspiration streaming down his face. "No, sir."

For the first time the girl turned from her father and faced Ronicky. She was not beautiful, but she was very pretty. Her hair was sand-colored and further faded by the sun. Constant exposure had tanned her dark bronze. But her big gray eyes were as bright and as steady as the torch in Ronicky's hand. There was something wonderfully honest and wonderfully feminine about her whole body and the carriage of her head. Ronicky guessed at once that here was a true Western girl who could ride like a man, shoot like a man, perhaps, and then at the end of the trail be gentleness itself. She was tensed with excitement as she looked to Ronicky now.

"Dad," she cried suddenly, "I believe every word he's spoken. His name is Doone. He has nothing to do with the band. And he's come here out of the honest goodness of his heart to warn you of Moon's intentions."

"Thanks, lady," said Ronicky. "It sure does me proud to hear you say that! Dawn, will you come to and see that what she says is the truth? I'll go one further. Now, Dawn, we're on even terms. Would one of Moon's men put you there?"

Hugh Dawn was staggered, for Ronicky had slipped his revolver back into his holster at his right hip. It was worse than an even break for Doone, because Dawn held in his hand, bared of the leather, the light thirty-two-caliber revolver which he had taken from the girl.

"Jerry," he said, "I dunno — I dunno. Moon's more full of tricks than a snake is of poison. But maybe this is square. Maybe this gent ain't got a thing to do with Moon."

"Then," cried Ronicky Doone, with a sudden passion, "for Heaven's sake act on it! Jump out of this house, saddle your hoss, and ride! Because Moon's coming!"

There was such honest eagerness in his voice that Hugh Dawn started as though to execute the suggestion. He only hesitated to say: "How come you to do all this riding and talking for me? What d'you get out of it? What am I to you?"

"You're a gent with four crooks on your heels," said Ronicky calmly. "I heard them talk. I couldn't let a murder be done if I could keep you from it. That's why I'm here."

The other shook his head. But the girl cried: "Don't you see, dad? He's simply — white! For Heaven's sake, believe him — trust in my trust. Get your things together. I'll saddle the gray and —"

The storm of her excited belief swept the other off his feet. He flashed one glance at Ronicky Doone, then turned on his heel and ran for his room.

The girl raced the other way, clattering down the stairs. Perhaps when she sprang outside into the night Jack Moon and his men would already be there. But she had never a thought for danger.

Ronicky Doone only delayed to run into the front room on that floor — the room from which the girl had spoken to him when he tried the front door — and there he lighted the lamp and placed it on the table near the window. After that he sped down the stairs, untethered Lou from her tree at the side of the house, and hurried with her to the back of the house and the old, tumble-down horseshed which stood there.

Lantern light showed there, where the girl was saddling a tall, gray gelding. She was working the cinch knots tight as Ronicky appeared, so fast had been her work, and now her father came from the house at a run, huddling himself into his slicker.

"How could they find out that I come here?" he asked. "After ten years!"

"No time for questions," his daughter said, panting. "Oh, dad, for Heaven's sake use the spurs tonight. Go back. Never return!"

"And leave you here alone?" asked Ronicky sternly. "Not when Moon and his gang are on the way. I seen their faces, lady, and they ain't a pretty lot! Leave you to be found by them? Not in a thousand years."

She grew a little pale at that, but she still kept her head high. "I've nothing to fear," she said. "They wouldn't dare harm me."

41

"I'll trust 'em dead, not living," said Ronicky. "You're going to ride with your father and on that hoss yonder!"

There was a companion to the gray, hardly so tall, but even better formed.

"He's right," said Hugh Dawn. As he spoke he caught saddle and bridle from their hooks and slapped them onto the horse. "I ain't thinking right to-night. I ain't understanding things. Doone, you put shame on me! Of course I ain't going to leave her alone!"

Ronicky heard these remarks with only half an ear.

He called from the door of the shed, where he had taken his stand: "Now put out the lantern! No use calling them this way with a light!"

He was hastily obeyed. Through the darkness they led out the two grays beside Lou.

"And you, Doone," said Hugh Dawn, who seemed to have been recovering his poise rapidly during the past seconds, "ride down the east road. We'll go over the hills. To-morrow Jerry can come back, when it's safe. And — Doone, shake hands! I forgive that punch that knocked me cold. Some day we —"

"Shut up," whispered Ronicky Doone impolitely and with savage force. "There they come!"

Four ghostly, silent figures, stooping low, advancing with stealthy stride, came out of the pines and slid toward the house. They could not be distinguished individually. They were simply blurs in the mist of rainfall, but for some reason their very obscurity made them more significant, more formidable. Ronicky Doone heard a queer, choked sound — Hugh Dawn swallowing a horror that would not down.

"And — and I near stayed there in the house and waited — for this!" he breathed.

Ronicky Doone jerked up a threatening fist. Not that there was a real danger that they might be overheard at that distance, but because he had odd superstitions tucked away in him here and there, and one of those superstitions was that words were more than mere sounds. They were thoughts that went abroad in an electric medium and possessed a life of their own. They might dart across a great space, these things called words. They might enter the minds and souls of men to whom they were not addressed. The idea had grown up in Ronicky Doone during long periods of silence in the mountains, in the desert where silence itself is a voice.

That raised fist brought the hunted man's teeth together with a snap. Then the gesture of Ronicky commanded them to go forward, on foot, leading their horses. He himself went last and acted as the rear guard while they trudged out past the horseshed — blessing the double night of its shadow! — and up the grade, then swerving around among the trees on the narrow uptrail which would eventually take them over the hills. They came even with the side of the house.

"Good Lord!" breathed Dawn. "They sure ain't got up that high already — but — they's a light in the front room — your room, Jerry!"

"I left that lamp," Ronicky Doone told them, grinning. "I thought it'd keep 'em nice and quiet for a while and make 'em sneak up to that door slow and easy, slow and easy — then pop! wide goes the door, and they run in and find — nothing!"

He laughed fiercely, silently — no sound coming save the light catching of his breath.

"You got a brain," said the rescued man.

"Heaven bless you!" whispered his daughter.

"We can climb the hosses now," said Ronicky, who seemed to have been admitted into the post of commander. "No danger of being seen. But ride slow. Things that move fast are seen a pile quicker than things that stand still. Now!"

He gave the example of swinging into the saddle on Lou. The girl, as she imitated, went up lightly as a feather, but Hugh Dawn's great bulk brought a loud grunt from the gray he bestrode, and the three sat a moment, straining in fear. But there was no sound. The four shadows had melted into the greater shadow of the house.

They began at a walk. They climbed higher on the swinging trail among the trees until they were above another eminence and looked down. The house seemed as near as ever, the trail had zigzagged so much to make the altitude. They could see the front of the building clearly, and suddenly the light wobbled, flashed to the side, and almost went out; then it grew dimmer in the center of the apartment.

"They've found out the trick," said Ronicky

44

Doone, speaking in a natural voice and chuckling.

"Hush!" panted the girl.

"We can talk out now, long's we don't do no shouting. They've sprung the trap, and they've got nothing! Not a thing!" He laughed again.

"Thanks to you, partner," said Hugh Dawn. "Thanks to you, lad!" There was a ring to his low voice.

The girl added a pleasant grace note to what her father had said: "To think," she said, "that when you spoke from the door — such a little time ago! — I was paralyzed with fear. I thought you were they. I thought they had come for dad! And — well, every day that he lives from now on, is a day due to you, Mr. Doone; and he will never forget. I will never forget."

For some reason that assurance that she would never forget meant more to Ronicky Doone than any assurance from the grown man.

"Look here," he said, "you don't owe nothing to me. It's Lou that done it. It's Lou that outfooted their hosses and give me the half hour's head start. She piled that up inside of twenty miles' running, too, and after she'd gone a weary way yesterday. Yep, if you got anything to thank, it's Lou. Me, I just done what anybody'd do. I'll leave you folks here," he added, as he got to the top of the crest of the hills with them.

"Leave us? Oh, no!" cried the girl and added hastily: "But of course. You see, I forget, Mr. Doone. It seems that so many things have happened to the three of us to-night that we are all bound together."

"I wish we were," said Hugh Dawn. "But you got your business, lad. Besides, I bring bad luck. Stay clear of me, or you'll have the bad luck, too!"

Ronicky's esteem of the man rose up the scale.

"Folks," he said kindly, "I'm one of them with nothing on my hands but a considerable lot of time and an itch for action. Seems to me that there may be some more action before this game's done and over, and I'd sort of like to horn in and have my say along with you, Dawn — if you want me and need me, I mean!"

Dawn answered: "It's on your own head, if you do. Doone, I'm in fear of death. But — need you? Why, man, I have the greatest thing in the world to do, and I'm single-handed in the doing of it. That's all. But if you'll take the chance, why, I'll trust you, and I'll let you in on the ground floor. But if you come with me, lad, you'll be taking the chances. You'll be playing for millions of dollars. But you'll be putting up your life in the gamble. How does that sound to you? But remember that if you come along with me, you get Jack Moon and his tribe of bloodhounds on your trail, and if they ever come up with you, you're dead. Understand?"

"Dad," cried the girl, "I'm burning with shame to hear you talk —"

"It's his concern!" declared her father. "Let him talk out. D'you know what I'm talking about? Millions, girl, millions — not just mere thousands! Millions in bullion!"

"Millions of fun," and Ronicky Doone laughed. "That's what it sounds like to me."

"Then," said the older man eagerly, "suppose we shake on it!"

"No, no!" cried Jerry Dawn. She even rode in between them.

"What d'you mean, Jerry?" asked her father impatiently.

"Oh," she said, "every one has tried the cursed thing, and every one has gone down; and now you take in the one generous and kind and pure-hearted man who has ever come into our lives. You take him, and you begin to drag him down in the net. Oh, dad, is this a reward for him? Is this a reward for him?"

There was almost a sob in her voice.

"Lady," said Ronicky Doone, "you're sure kind, but I've made up my mind. Remember that story about Bluebeard's wife? She had all the keys but one, and she plumb busted her heart because she couldn't get that one key and see inside that one room. Well, lady, the same's true with me. Suppose I had the key to everything else in the world and just this one thing was left that I could get at; well, I'd turn down all the other things in the world that I know about and take to this one thing that I don't know anything about, just because I don't know it. Danger? Well, lady, danger is the finest bait in the world for any gent like me that's fond of action and ain't never been fed full

47

on it. That's the straight of it."

"Then," said the girl sadly, "Heaven forgive us for bringing this down on your generous heart!" And she drew her horse back.

The two men reached through the dark night and the rain. Their wet, cold hands fumbled, met, and closed in a hard grasp. It was like a flash of light, that gripping of the hands. It showed them each other's minds as a glint of light would have shown their faces.

# CHAPTER VI

## A PAUSE FOR REST

As the trio plodded on steadily through the night, many things about the father and daughter impressed Ronicky Doone favorably.

There was something so fine, so naturally well-bred about their whole attitude, that he felt his heart warming to both; and yet there were reasons enough for him to maintain an attitude of suspicion and caution so far as the pair was concerned. He was calling the girl "Jerry" before the ride was ended; both father and daughter were calling him "Ronicky." Those were the chief conversational results of that night.

The ride lasted all the night and well on into the morning. Lou, great-heart that she was, bore up wonderfully. She had the endurance of an Arab horse, and indeed she resembled an Arab in her stanch and tapering build. The big grays struck a hard pace and kept to it, but Lou matched them with her smooth-flowing gait. Her head went down a little as time passed, but when the dawn came, gray and cold under a rainless sky, it showed her still with an ample reserve of strength, while the grays were well-nigh as fagged as though they had covered all her distance of miles in the past twenty-four hours.

For the sake of Ronicky's horse, knowing the distance the mare had covered, the Dawns would have stopped the journey for rest, but Ronicky would not hear of it. As he pointed out, Jack Moon could not attempt to pick up the trail until the morning; and then he probably would only be able to locate it by striking out in a great circle with the house as the center of his sweeping radius. If they pushed straight ahead, stopping only when they had put a solid day's march behind them, they would doubtless pass well beyond the reach of that radius, particularly since the outlaws would be looking for the signs of two horses instead of three. These reasons were so patent that they were accepted, and so the party held on its way.

By midmorning they came in sight of a village among the hills to their left. Ronicky — because he would not be recognized by Moon's scouts in case they inquired after Dawn in that place — rode down into the town and bought supplies; then he rejoined the group on the trail four miles out from the village, and they pressed on for another hour. The sight of a little ruined shack here proved too strong a temptation for them, and they determined to make their day's halt. They were too tired to prepare a meal. Canned beans, crackers, and coffee were their portion. They slept wrapped in their blankets.

At four in the afternoon Ronicky wakened to find that Hugh Dawn was already up. He had kindled a fire in the wrecked stove which, without a chimney, stood in one corner of the shack; and now he sat beside it, his hands wrapped about his knees, a big black pipe clenched between his teeth, and his eyes fixed, through the doorway, upon the south trail. The broad shoulders, which could not be pulled forward even by the draw of the arms in this position; the forward thrust of the heavy head and the powerful neck; the solemn and alert expression of the face — all of these things went to convince Ronicky, as he lay unstirring for a moment in his blankets, that his new-found companion was by no means a soft variety of adventurer. The night before he had shown himself in the most unfavorable, and almost a cowardly, light. But no doubt that was explained as a result of a long hounding — explained by the fact that he was returning from safety into a region where his life would constantly be in danger.

Ronicky could not help admiring the quiet with which the man had been able to light the fire and break up wood and handle the noisy plates of the stove without making sufficient disturbance to waken either him — a remarkably light sleeper at all times — or the girl.

She lay in the position she had taken when she first wrapped herself in the blankets, her face turned up and pillowed in the tumbled masses of her hair. But on her lips, strangely enough, there was the smile of complete happiness and joyous dreams. Ronicky saw the face of the father, as it turned for an instant to the girl, soften wonderfully and lose every stern line. Again his heart warmed to the man.

He sat up in his blankets, was greeted by a smile and a silent raising of the hand, and, after folding his blanket, went outside to find water. He discovered a place a hundred yards away, where a little freshet had pooled its waters in a small lake, and that tempted him to a swim. He came back from his bath and shave, and saw that the father had not changed his position. Only iron muscles and a mind wrapped in the profoundest meditations could have kept him in that cramping posture.

At sight of Ronicky he rose, and, crossing the rotted boards of the floor with marvelous softness, considering his bulk, he came out to greet his new friend.

"What I been thinking," he said, after he had drawn Ronicky far enough away to be out of earshot of the girl, "is that we better get ready for a start and go on, leaving Jerry a note to say that she's better at the house than she is with us. What do you think of that?"

"Only one thing," said Ronicky Doone, after a moment of consideration. "Does Jerry know where you're bound?"

"In a general way she does."

"Then," said Ronicky, "if she knows in a general way, she's apt to follow on and try to find us. Or, if she doesn't do that, she'll go back to the big house and die of loneliness, wondering what's happening to you. And at the house, who knows if Moon won't drop in on her, and take some means of finding out from her where you've gone — eh?"

"It'd take torture to get that out of her."

"That's just what I mean."

Hugh Dawn started.

Ronicky explained: "I only saw his face once. You must know him a pile better than I do. But I got this to say, that if ever I saw a cold-blooded devil in the form of a man, Jack Moon is him. Am I right?"

"A thousand times right!" and Hugh Dawn sighed. "But I've been so long away — I've looked back on the West as a place where women at least are sacred — that I plumb forgot what a fiend Moon is. Ronicky, you're correct. We can't leave the girl. But if we take her with us, won't she run into the same danger?"

"No, because if she's with us she'll not have any information to give Moon — nothing to be browbeaten about or hurt. I take it that if he finds us where we're going, he'll know everything."

"I guess so," said the older man, knotting his brows anxiously.

"Unless," suggested Ronicky, "you can afford to send her back and get the protection of the law for her; but I gather that you don't want to bring yourself to the notice of the law much more than you want to bring yourself to the notice of Jack Moon."

"Right!" The big man nodded sadly. "That's just the place I stand in. Poor Jerry! Ronicky, they's a curse on this treasure we're after. Maybe

53

Jerry's right. I was all wrong to bring you in on it. But, playing my lone hand, I was pretty sure I could never beat Moon. With you I figured that we'd all have a chance — of being rich!"

Ronicky nodded.

"And I suppose you want to know something, Ronicky, about me and the treasure and Moon and all?"

"I want to know just as much as comes easy for you to tell me, Dawn."

"To begin with, what d'you know already?"

"Only bits that I gathered, which round up to something like this: That once you belonged to Moon's crowd. That you broke away from the crowd ten years ago. That in Moon's crew the punishment for desertion is death. That you ran out of the country to keep clear of him. That he worked hard to get on your trail all the time. That the minute you got back, he learned about it. That he's trying to kill you now. That you came back here partly because you wanted to see the girl. That another thing brought you back, which was this treasure you talk about. That's as much as I know, or think I know. Am I right? Mind you, I ain't asking for a thing that comes hard for you to tell. Every gent has shadowy places in his life. I have 'em. Everybody has 'em." The other man drank in the words hungrily.

"What you've said," he declared eagerly, "makes it plumb easy to talk to you compared with anybody else I've ever knowed. I've only got this to say, that I'm going to make a clean breast of everything to you. It'll take time, but we got time. Jerry needs another hour for rest. Girls ain't like men. They get plumb no-good unless they have their sleep. Speaking of Jerry, I got to say that she don't know the half of what I'm going to tell you — and I don't expect her ever to learn anything more from you."

"Partner," said Ronicky, "I understand."

# CHAPTER VII

## THE TREASURE TALE

Dawn cast about in his mind for an easy method of opening a rather difficult narrative. It was essential that he should not lose the respect of his new-found ally; for he sensed at once the vital truth that Ronicky Doone could not work for an instant with a companion whom he did not trust.

At length he hit upon a lucky beginning and pointed down the hillside.

"You see that old pine tree down there on the side of the hill among the rocks?" he said.

"Yes."

"And you see that other one on the level shoulder? Well, one of 'em is packed in among rocks and hasn't a square chance to grow; and even when it grows, it pitches out to the side, all crooked. And the other goes up big and straight as a king, eh? Ronicky, it's the same way with humans. Take two men of the same kind and give one a chance and one a hard row. One of 'em goes straight, the other goes crooked. Well, Ronicky, that's my case.

"My father built that big house you saw last night, and I grew up in it. He was a money-maker;

an easy-going fellow, too; and he liked to spend money as well as he liked to make it. Mines were his meat, and you know how cheap you regard gold that you dig out of dirt. He treated me the same way he treated himself. I grew up just the way I felt like growing. He didn't make me do anything. I didn't feel like going off to school, and he didn't make me. Result was that I just ran wild, got to be a man, married the finest girl that ever stepped, had a girl born — and then the mines went smash, and dad went smash with them. Left me stranded. I didn't have any occupation. I didn't know anything about ranch work, even. And how was I to support my family? Then came a hard winter. My father and my wife died and left me with the baby girl to take care of. That hit me pretty hard. When your wife goes hungry it's bad enough; but when a kid cries for food, it sure cuts you up.

"I started out to get coin. And I got it! Tried my hand at gambling, and I had a beginner's luck that lasted me two years. Then that luck petered out, and I was flat as ever — and nothing saved of all the money I'd made.

"When I was down and out, Jack Moon met me. He'd been watching me for a long time like the fox that he is. He saw me going downhill and he waited for the right time. When it came, he was ready. He put up his game to me, and I fell for it. I was desperate, you see? And the way he told me was that I wouldn't have to ride with him more'n a couple of times a year. The only hard thing was that, once in the band, I had to stay with it all my life. But even that I was willing to do, because there was Jerry, nearly eight years old, pretty as a picture, and needing a pile of things to keep her happy. So I gave Moon my word and went in with him.

"He didn't call on me for six months. Meantime, he gave me money, kept me easy, and built up a big debt that I owed him. End of the six months he called on me. It was a safe-blowing job. I rode with Moon and two others, and I didn't do much but look on; but afterward I got a split on the profits. Well, Ronicky, that night when I saw the soup explode and the door of the safe blown off, it seemed to me I was seeing the whole power of the law blown to the devil. It was more'n I could stand. I got Moon aside and told him that I was pretty well tired of the whole thing and I wanted to turn in my share to pay off my debts to him and get myself out of the band. But Moon only laughed at me. He said that every man was a little hard hit his first time out, but afterward he got used to it. Besides, he said that I had the makings of a new leader, if anything happened to him; and he tried to flatter me into being happy.

"It didn't work, but he said enough to show me that he'd never let me get out of his control. That started me thinking faster and harder than I'd ever thought before.

"About two months later he called on me. I can see now that he simply wanted to test me out. He said he knew that I was a hard rider and a good shot, and he said, too, that he was going to honor me by giving me the job of running down a skunk that had tried to double-cross his band. This was the story that Moon told me, and I'll try to give you every point just as he gave 'em to me.

"A good many years back, they made the gold strikes along the Jervey River — you've heard about 'em?"

"Of course!" Ronicky nodded.

"Well, those strikes were about the richest ever made, according to what Moon told me. The boys dug out the gold like dirt. They got it by the millions. It was all surface stuff, and the claims gave out quick; but while they lasted — about two years and a half — they were mints. The chief trouble with the mines along the Jervey was that they wasn't any railroad within three hundred miles, and the gold had to be carted out on mules and hosses along the trails across the mountains. Naturally there was a lot of robbing and holdups going on — such a pile of it that nobody could say how much gold was lost or how many men murdered in the business. But Jack Moon says that out of about sixty millions taken from the Jervey claims, not more'n twenty millions ever was got across the mountains by them that shipped it out!

"Forty millions was lost. Think of that! You'd think that losses like that would have brought out the whole United States army to look after things. But the whole army wasn't very big in those days, and it was tolerable busy with the Indians. Besides, when the stories got East, they weren't believed; or if they were believed, nobody cared very much. They were used to hearing all kinds of wild tales about gold coming out of the West, and most generally they figured that the gold diggers were a set of rascals, one about as bad as the other. So nothing was done till the miners done it.

"They bore up for a long time, until after a while pretty nigh none of the gold ever got across the mountains. Then they stopped digging and got ready to fight, and they were about as good at one thing as the other. They meant trouble, and they meant trouble in heaps. In a couple of weeks something broke. They sent out a fake gold convoy. There wasn't any gold, but there were ten mules and only ten men — and behind the ten came close to fifty with rifles. Sure enough, the ten were jumped, there was a big fight, and half a dozen of the robbers were shot down. The miners were so mad that they didn't leave 'em live long. But one gent kept a spark of life, and he lived long enough to tell 'em that the whole system of robbing was run under one head, and that that head was the gent that was sheriff of the district where the mines was! The skunk had worked a double game and won both ways. His name was Hampden.

"Them fifty men went back to the claims and rounded up Hampden. At first he put up quite a talk; but they faced him with the dying gent, and he weakened. He was smooth as oil, but there was some things that he couldn't answer. When they searched his cabin and found under the flooring some guns that was known to belong to gents that had been murdered on the gold trails, they give that sheriff a short time for living.

"His nerve held good till they tied the knot around under his ear and got him ready for the swing, and then he buckled. He begged 'em to give him a chance. He swore that he wasn't any more than a tool; and that the gent that had planned all the organized robbery was really to blame, and that if they'd spare his life he'd take them to that gent and they could not only get him that was the root of the whole affair, but they could get the gold that had been stolen — a third or half of it, anyway, because that was the share, he said, that the master kept for himself.

"Of course the vigilantes figured this talk to be just plumb fear. Hampden wanted to live, and so he was lying and putting the blame on somebody that didn't exist. Anyway, they cut him short by kicking the box from under him, and Hampden swung still trying to talk and explain as long as he had a breath in him.

"Now let's go back to Jack Moon. He heard about this story; and he had an idea that they was something in it. Seems he hunted around for ten years trying to locate who the master mind had been, if there was such a man; and finally he hit on a gent named Boyd Cosslett that lived in a cabin right up on a cliff over the Cunningham River. He was a queer old gent with yards of white beard, and always packing the Bible around and living

61

quiet. What started the suspicions of Moon was that no letters and no money ever come in for old Boyd Cosslett, but every now and then he went down to town and bought supplies, and what he paid down was always raw gold or dust!

"Well, Moon had him watched for nigh onto a year, trying to see if the old boy would ever leave his cabin and go out to his treasure — if he really had a treasure buried some place. But nothing happened, so one day he took a couple of the boys, Whitwell and another, and rushed Cosslett's shack at night.

"The old miser must of had the ears of a fox. He heard 'em coming. When they smashed through the door, they found him closing something into an iron box on the table. Moon shot him twice with his revolver, but Cosslett lived long enough to snap his box shut and throw it into the river. Then he turned around and laughed and shook his fist at Moon and dropped.

"They looked out the window and saw that the box must of fallen straight over the cliff and down into the lake, because that's the place where the Cunningham River widens out and fills the ravine and makes Cunningham Lake.

"Cosslett lived about an hour, and Moon tried to make him talk; but the old boy just lay reading his Bible out loud and waiting for death.

"After he died, they buried him all proper. Moon's a stickler for things like that. Then they went down and dragged the lake to get the iron box, because they figured that it must contain something they could use as a clew to finding the treasure. But the bottom of that lake was thick with mud, and they got nothing but tired arms for their work.

"Now, about a month after this Whitwell disappeared, and they didn't find him for a long time. And he stayed away so long that Moon knew he had quit the band. After a while they pick up his trail and find him not far from Cosslett's cabin. And there they find him dragging the lake!

"It's easy to figure what he was doing. He was trying to get his hands on that iron box of old Cosslett's and he wanted to get it for himself and not have to share up with the band. Moon let him stay on there for a month, hoping that maybe Whitwell would find the box; and then they'd kill Whitwell and take the box from him. But Whitwell didn't have any luck, it seemed, so finally Moon came to me and gave me the job of killing Whitwell.

"I tried to beg out of it, but there was nothing to do but go and kill or else get killed myself. That was the rule under Jack Moon, and that's the rule under him still.

"When I reached Cunningham Lake, I found that Whitwell was gone; but I picked up a fresh trail and followed it two days. It brought me up at last to an old deserted camp, and there I nailed Whitwell. There wasn't anything to it. He was sound asleep in a chair. When he woke up, I had my gun shoved under his chin.

"Well, he didn't even so much as blink. He just

sat up and grinned at me. First thing he said was: 'I'm ready to divvy up, if that's what you want.'

" 'Divvy up on what?' I asked him.

" 'The box,' says he. 'I found it.'

"That took my breath. I'd heard so much from Moon, he seemed so sure that that box held the clew to the treasure, that I gaped at Whitwell. He went on to talk smooth and easy. He figured that I'd come along for him. He admitted that I had him, and that I could blow his head off, but what was the good? I told him, and I told him true, that I couldn't kill him, that the job had been forced on me, and that I hated Moon and the rest of his band. That was music to Whitwell. He told me the whole story right off. He'd found the box by dragging. But it was heavy; weighed forty pounds, even if it was small. He tried to break it open, but he didn't have a sledge hammer; and while he was trying to smash the lock against a rock he saw somebody coming up the river road. He took his glasses and made out that it was me.

"He knew, of course, why I was after him. He saddled and jumped onto his horse. But he couldn't take that heavy box with him, so he left it behind at Cosslett's house and then tore off across the hills. What he intended to do was to shake me off the trail, get some giant powder, return and blow up the box, and then see what was to be seen.

"Now he offered to share everything with me. I thanked him, and we were shaking hands to seal the bargain when a gun was fired through the win-

64

dow, and Whitwell was shot out of his chair.

"Of course Moon had just been trying me out, and when he sent me on the trail he sent a tried man after me to see what I did. He had orders to simply kill me if I tried to dodge the work. And that was what his man tried to do, because the second Whitwell spilled out of his chair, another shot was sent at me and just clipped through my hair. I dropped to the floor beside Whitwell. My ear was close to his lips. I heard him whisper: 'Under the veranda,' and then he was dead.

"In the meantime, the front door of the cabin opened, and big Si Treat came in. He figured that he'd killed us both with those two shots, from the way we'd both dropped. There was nothing for it but to get him out of the way. I shot for his legs, saw him go down, and then I scrambled through the door and rode like mad for Cunningham Lake.

"But I never got there. Treat hadn't come alone. Moon and two others were with him, and they rode like devils to cut me off. They did it and turned me into the south mountains. For a month they hunted me, and for a month I managed to keep out of bullet range. By that time I was away south, and I saw that the country was too hot for me. I could never get back to Jerry. They'd watch around her and lay for me. There was only one thing left, and that was to get as far away as I could, start to work, and support Jerry.

"I couldn't send for her, because the minute she left that devil Moon would trail her to me. I just had to live where I was and work and send her the money to live on. And that's what I did. Ten years of it, lad, without ever seeing her face. But I gave her enough for an education. Then when she was independent I made up my mind that I'd come back and risk the chance to get Cosslett's gold. I came back then, told Jerry simply that I was in danger from Moon and his band, and started to plan to get to Cunningham Lake and Cosslett's old shack. But before I got well started, you know what happened. You arrived in time to drag me out to safety. You arrived in time to give me a fighting chance at that money — and give yourself a chance at the same thing!"

"And Jerry knows —"

"Only that we're trying to get that iron box. She knows the story behind that, and how Moon killed the old man. She knows that I can't call down the law on the head of Moon because there are complications; but just what those complications are, she can't say. Is it all clear to you now, Ronicky, just how we stand?"

"All clear, I guess," said Doone. "But it looks to me as though there's a trail of crimson spilled all around that gold of Cosslett's. First men were killed so that he could get his hands on it. Then other gents were bumped off because they were his agents. Then Cosslett was killed because he had the gold; and then several other gents were killed because they were trying to find out where Cosslett hid the stuff. Now here we go, you and me, and take your girl with us; and all three of us walk up and rap at the same door. Well, Dawn, it looks like black business to me!"

"You're losing heart, Ronicky?" asked the elder man gloomily.

"I'll stay with it as long as the next man," declared Ronicky. "One thing I'd like to know. Won't Moon suspect that we're heading for Cosslett's old shack? Won't he be apt to drive straight for that place and wait for us there?"

"It's a chance," said Hugh Dawn, "but that's a chance we got to take. Moon don't know Whitwell's secret. I'm the only one that knows it except you and Jerry."

"But if he strikes around blind for the trail and doesn't find it," said Ronicky, "he might start straight for Cosslett's, and then we'd simply be running into the trap. Besides, maybe he guesses that you know something."

"He guesses that Whitwell knew something, and that Whitwell told me. What it is, he can't guess. But if he's at Cosslett's — then that's fate. And if fate's agin' us, we'll be beat any way we look at it. But we won't be beat, son. I feel lucky! We can get to Cosslett's inside of two hours of hard riding. And Moon ain't apt to get there as quick as that. Then a look under the veranda —"

"But what if somebody else has looked there in the last ten years?"

"Not a chance. That veranda was built close to the ground. If Whitwell put it there, he must have put it there because he knew nobody'd look there."

"Then, Hugh, we'll start."

"Yes. Jerry has rested enough by this time!"

# CHAPTER VIII

## AT COSSLETT'S CABIN

It seemed to Ronicky that there was more than an ordinary admixture of superstition in the nature of Hugh Dawn. If fate aided him, he would get Cosslett's gold. If fate were against him, he would get death instead. So he went ahead blindly trusting in luck. He had made only one sensible provision to meet danger, and that was enlisting the aid of another man, Ronicky himself. The more Ronicky thought of the affair, the more of a wild-goose chase it seemed to him.

Yet he knew that it was madness to attempt to dissuade Hugh Dawn, and he dared not let the big fellow go on with his daughter to face Moon. And face the outlaw chief he knew they would, before the adventure was finished.

Returning to the cabin, they found Geraldine Dawn already up, and they found, moreover, that she had reached the conclusion to which they had already come. She dared not go back and live alone in the big house of her father; a thousand times she would rather continue the trip and face whatever lay before them, than make the return.

Only one thing upset her — what would the

people of Trainor say when she did not appear to teach the school? But there was, in the village, a girl who had substituted for her once before during an illness. Therefore the classes would be taken care of. With that scruple cared for — how slight a thing it seemed to Ronicky Doone! — she was ready to face the adventure.

They started on within a few minutes, swerving now to the left and striking through rougher mountain trails. Hugh Dawn had correctly estimated the distance. In the early evening they came upon Cosslett's cabin.

It stood in an imposing place on the cliff above Cunningham Lake. On all sides the ground sloped back. There were no trees near, though in all other directions the forest stepped down from the mountaintops to the very edge of the lake.

"You see?" exclaimed Hugh Dawn. "The old boy picked a place where he could look on all sides of him. He wouldn't trust a forest where gents could sneak up on him."

Ronicky smiled to himself. Such reasoning simply proved that Dawn had already convinced himself, and was willing to pick up minute circumstances and weave them into the train of proof.

They climbed the slope and found that ten years had dealt hard with the little house. The roof was smashed in. The sides caved out, as though the pressure of time were overcoming them. But the first place to which they ran, the veranda, showed no opening beneath its floor and the ground.

Hugh Dawn looked at it in despair. The ground,

indeed, was flush with the top of the flooring.

"I must of remembered wrong," he muttered, "but it seems to me that in the old days they used to be a space between the floor and the hill. I dunno how this come!"

Ronicky had been surveying the site carefully.

"Maybe the house had settled," he suggested. "We'll tear up the boards and see."

It was easily done. The rotted wood gave readily around the nail-heads, and in a minute or two every board had been torn up. But they saw beneath no sign of such a thing as a forty-pound iron chest. Hugh Dawn was in despair.

"Maybe somebody else has lived here and found it and —"

He could not complete the sentence, so great was his disappointment. Ronicky, expecting nothing at all, was quite unperturbed. He looked at Jerry Dawn. She was as calm as he, but something of pity was in her eyes as she looked to her father. Was it possible that she, too, saw through the whole hoax and had simply undertaken the ride to appease the hungry eagerness of her father?

"We'll go inside," she suggested.

They entered the cabin through the front doorway, stepping over the door itself, which had fallen on the inside. All within was at the point of disintegration. The cast-iron stove was now a red, rusted heap in a corner. The falling of a rafter had smashed the bunk where it was built against the wall. The boards of the floor gave and creaked beneath their steps. In the corners were little yellow heaps of paper — old letters, they seemed. And on the floor beneath the bunk Jerry Dawn found, face down, and yet with every page intact, the Bible which was always mentioned whenever the name of Cosslett was brought into conversation.

When she raised the book, it seemed that she raised the ghost of the old white-bearded hermit at the same time. In spite of the ruin, the terrible scene rushed back upon the memory of each of the three — Jack Moon and his men tumbling through the door — the two explosions of guns — the hurling of the casket through the window — the fall of the hermit.

Suddenly Hugh Dawn shouted in alarm. Making a careless step, his great weight had driven his foot crashing and rending through the flooring where rain had rotted away the wood except for a mere shell. He scrambled out of his trap, half laughing and half alarmed.

"The old gent had a cellar," said Ronicky, "judging by the way your leg went through that floor."

Jerry Dawn looked up from the Bible, whose yellowed, time-stained leaves she had been turning with reverent fingers. The awe went out of her eyes, and bright interest came in its place.

"A cellar?" she asked. "Then let's look at it. Perhaps that's the place where he hid all the gold, dad?"

Her father snorted.

"Are you trying to make a joke out of this?"

he asked heavily. "Hide the gold in the cellar! Hide fifteen or twenty million dollars' worth of gold in a cellar!"

"Twenty millions?" gasped Ronicky, beginning to fear for the sanity of his companion. "Are you serious about that, Dawn?"

"Why not? The band must of took a clean forty millions, and out of everything that they took, that old hawk, according to Hampden, got fifty per cent. He was a business man, right enough! And what's half of forty? Twenty millions, boy!"

That hungry glittering came into his glance again, and Ronicky shook his head.

"But we'll see about the cellar." He nodded to Jerry Dawn.

She leaned to see him put his fingers through a gaping crack between boards, work them to a firm grip, and then rip up the whole length of the plank. Below them opened the black depth of the cellar. Ronicky lighted a match and dropped it into the aperture.

"Six foot of hole," he announced. "Down I go!"

Two more boards were torn away, and he prepared to lower himself.

"But what good does all that foolishness do?" groaned the despairing fortune hunter. "If the box ain't under the veranda —"

"Ladies bring luck," answered Ronicky, grinning. "I'm going to follow her orders every time I get a chance."

And down he dropped into the hole.

"Ever hear of such crazy work?" growled the father.

But Jerry was becoming interested in the fate of her own suggestion.

"Who'd put a box like that in a cellar!" exclaimed Hugh Dawn. "Who'd do that — put it right out in plain view!"

"Plain view? Who suspected a cellar under a house like this until you put your foot through the floor?"

Ronicky was lighting matches in the darkness below. Presently he called: "I see how come the veranda to be down to the ground level. All the stringers holding up the floor on this side are rotten and smashed over sidewise. And —"

He stopped.

"We're beat," said Hugh Dawn, "before we get fairly started. I've come back and put my head into the mouth of the lion for nothing. That skunk Whitwell aimed to make a fool of me, that was all! Why should he of told me the truth, anyway?"

"Because dying men don't lie!" shouted Ronicky Doone through the hole in the floor, and at the same time he cast up what looked like a great, rectangular chunk of rust. It fell with a crash onto the floor, the jar of the impact knocking off from its sides long flakes of the red dust, so that the metal looked forth from beneath.

Ronicky vaulted up through the hole and stood exultant beside them.

"He did put it under the veranda!" he cried. "He put it so far under that it rolled right on down

74

into the cellar. And there it's laid ever since!"

They stood about it in trembling excitement, Jerry so agape with astonishment that it was plain she had considered, up to this point, that the whole story was a myth. Hugh Dawn was beyond use of his muscles. Only Ronicky Doone had not been incapacitated by wonder and excitement.

For unquestionably it was the "forty-pound box" so often referred to. Even Ronicky Doone was convinced. Of course there was no reason to think that the box proved anything, or that its discovery led to important things. But as it stood there in the center of the three, a mass of red rust, its presence verified one step in the story of the Cosslett treasure, and thereby the whole trail seemed to be the truth. The rotting strong box was like a fourth presence. Its silence was more eloquent than a voice.

# CHAPTER IX

## THE IRON BOX

"It's heavy enough to have a tidy bunch of gold in it," said Ronicky. "Let's get her open. Did you bring a sledge hammer, Dawn?"

The latter looked at him reproachfully.

"Figure I'd come on a trip like this without getting a pack ready long before? Nope, Ronicky, I had my pack under my arm when I left the house on the run last night, and the things in the pack are a pick and a shovel and a chisel and an eight-pound sledge."

As he enunciated the last word Ronicky disappeared through the door. Hugh Dawn picked up the strong box and, carrying it outside, had braced it firmly, lock up, between two big stones ready for the hammering which was to open it. Ronicky came a moment later with the hammer.

"Now," Hugh cried, brandishing the hammer about his head, "look sharp!"

He loosed a terrific blow which landed fairly and squarely upon the lock. But the hammer, after crunching through the rust, rebounded idly. The lock had not even been cracked. He whirled it again, again, and again. His back went up and down, and the sledge became a varying streak of light that struck against the box, always hitting accurately on one spot. Ronicky Doone looked on in amazement, and the girl's eyes shone in delight at the prowess of her father, when there was a slight sound of cracking; at another blow the box flew open.

Inside there were exposed a few scraps of paper, and nothing else!

Ronicky Doone gasped with excitement. Was it true, then, that what the box was used for, was to guard a secret and not money?

Hugh Dawn, panting with labor and joy, gathered the paper fragments in trembling fingers.

"Read 'em, Jerry," he said. "I — my eyes are all blurred. Where's the map, first off?"

There were three slips of paper, apparently fly leafs of books torn off, and the girl examined them.

"There's no map," she said. "I'm sorry, dad."

"No map!" he shouted. "Let me see! Let me see!"

He snatched them from her, glaring; then he crumpled the paper into a ball and cast it to the ground.

"No wonder Cosslett died with a smile," he groaned. "It was only a joke that he locked up in that box and threw away so careful. If ghosts walk the earth, he's somewhere in the air now laughing at me." He looked up as though he half expected to see the old face take form out of the empty atmosphere.

"Nothing but a list of names and some figuring,"

the girl said with a sigh. "I'm afraid it was only a jest."

Ronicky Doone alone had not seen the writing. He ran a few steps after the ball of paper as it rolled along in the breeze, picked it up, and smoothed out the separate bits. What he found was exactly what had been reported. First there were two slips covered with a list of names and dates:

H. L. L. — September 22.
Gregory — May 9.
Scottie — August 14.

The list continued, each separate name followed by dates ranging through two years until October of the second year. With this month the dates were crowded together. Half of the first slip and all of the second were covered with names and dates of that month. And last of all was the name "Hampden, October 19."

It struck a faint light in Ronicky's groping imagination.

"Hampden was the gent that run the affair for Cosslett, wasn't he?" he asked.

"What of it?"

"Here's his name the last of the lot."

"And what does that mean?" Hugh Dawn asked.

Jerry Dawn came and peered with interest over the shoulder of Ronicky.

"It goes to prove that we're working on more than hearsay," the girl said. "Goes to prove that there was really a connection between Cosslett and Hampden, and in that case, why, Cosslett is simply a murderous old miser who used other men to do killings so that he could get gold, and who then sat down with his Bible and thought about his ill-gotten gains."

"I knew all that before," declared her father. "But this is a blank trail, Jerry. Cosslett's gold will rest and rot. No man'll ever find it — all them millions!"

Ronicky turned to the third slip. It was a compact jumble of figures. He read as follows:

(1, 1, 3, 2; 1, 1, 6, 5; 1, 1, 9, 1; 1, 1, 12, 5)
(2, 9, 1, 13; 2, 9, 1, 4; 2, 9, 3, 6)

So it ran on through line after line of bracketed numbers with commas and semicolons interspersed.

Ronicky Doone dropped the paper to his side. "Dawn," he said, "I figure that every word you've said is right, except where you begin to give up hope. But this mess of figures — I dunno what could have been in Cosslett's head when he started to make it up. Anyway, it can't do us any good."

He was about to throw the papers to the wind, but the girl stayed his hand.

"Just a moment," she said hastily, and, taking the slip which contained the figures, she perused it carefully.

Ronicky and her father anxiously turned toward her. Since both of them were convinced that the trail to the treasure began at the shack of Cosslett, and since there was no possible clew save that piece of paper and the list of numbers, they hoped against hope that Jerry could make something out of it.

"If they's any sense to it," said her father, "Jerry'll get at it. She always was a wonder at puzzles, even when she was no bigger'n a minute."

The girl raised her fine head, and now the gray eyes were glinting with excitement.

"It's a message of some kind written in a code," she announced. "There's no doubt about that."

The two men crowded about her.

"You see?" she pointed out. "There are thirteen of those bracketed groups. Inside the brackets the numbers are separated with commas and grouped with semicolons. I counted the groups set off by the semicolons, and altogether there are fifty-eight of them. Well, the average length of a word is about five letters. Five goes into fifty-eight eleven times and a little over. That's near enough. Fifty-eight letters to make up eleven words. And those eleven words — since they were locked up so carefully in the strong box — may they not form the directions to the place where the treasure is buried? I admit that I don't see how he could have written complete directions with so few words; but at least it gives us a new hope, doesn't it?"

The cheer from the two men was answer enough.

"After all," said Ronicky, "that leaves us almost as much in the dark as ever. See any way you can get at the code?"

"I don't know," said the girl, shaking her head. "It looks hard. But then, most puzzles seem hard until you get at them, you know; and, once they're deciphered, they seem so simple that every one is surprised he didn't see through the thing before. There are lots of ways of making up codes, of course. The oldest way is the worst. You simply substitute particular characters for the different letters. In that way you simply have a new alphabet."

"That sounds hard enough to suit me," said her father, peering anxiously over her shoulder at the paper.

"But, you see," explained Geraldine, "that there are ways of distinguishing letters by the frequency with which they are used. E is used much more than any other letter. Then come T, A, N, O, I, et cetera, in that same order. And —"

"Where in the world," broke in Ronicky Doone, "did you learn all that?"

"She's had a pile of schooling," replied the proud father.

"Not schooling," Jerry Dawn said, with a laugh. "It's just that I've always been interested in puzzles, and I've picked up odds and ends of information that way. But to come back to this conundrum. It obviously isn't one of the simple types of codes. I'm certain that each group inside a semicolon represents a letter, and not one of the groups is identical with another. So the 'substituted alphabet' code isn't used at all. Outside of that code, there are scores of others, of course. Any one can make up a code with a little forethought, and probably each code will be quite unlike, in several features, any other code in the world."

"Then we're through," said her father bitterly. He wiped the perspiration from his forehead.

"Please give me a chance to think," pleaded the girl, with a touch of irritation. "It isn't absolutely hopeless. At least there's room for work. For instance, inside of each bracket the first letter of each group is the same. And in each succeeding bracket the first letter is one larger. The characters of the first bracket run one, one, three, two; one, one, six, five; et cetera. In the second bracket they run two, nine, one, thirteen; two, nine, one, four; et cetera. And this continues right down to the last bracket, where the first character is thirteen."

"But what on earth does that show?"

"It shows an amateur maker of codes," said the girl firmly. "He could have left out the first character in every instance and found it simply by getting the number of the bracket in each case. Isn't that clear? But let's look at some other interesting features. The first character in each group is the same throughout the individual bracket. The second character is also identical throughout each bracket. In the first bracket the second character is everywhere one; in the second it is nine; in the third it is eighteen; in the fourth it is six. Each group is made up of four characters. The first two are regular throughout and follow some definite plan. The third character varies in the first two brackets only. In the first it is three, six, nine, twelve. In the second it is one, one, three. But after that the third character also becomes regular. In the third bracket it is always two, and in the fourth bracket it is always two; while in other brackets other numerals are used, but each is constant throughout the individual bracket. But the fourth character in each group is the variant. It changes continually."

"It all sounds like Greek to me," said Ronicky.

"I suppose it does," said the girl, "but that's simply because you haven't worked over things like this before. The regularity of the first three characters of the groups shows me that they are intended as guides. But the actual distinguishing element in each group is the last or fourth character. All of this, I admit, goes for nothing unless I get at some clew to the problem."

"Maybe we can help," suggested Ronicky, "when it comes to clews."

"They are of all kinds," said the girl, "these clews I refer to. They come out of the character and life of the man who makes the code, as a rule. This man, so far as I know, was a clever criminal. He also was fond of isolation and the Bible. Perhaps he thought he could read his way out of guilt and responsibility for his sins. At any rate, I'm going to think over what I know about him. The whole thing may clear up in a moment."

And she walked away meditatingly tapping the Bible which had belonged to the dead Cosslett.

"She's got book, chapter, and verse," Ronicky Doone remarked, with a grin, "and, as long as she's that far along she'll find the words pretty soon."

These words were hardly out of his mouth when the girl turned on him in a flash.

"Do you mean that seriously?" she cried eagerly.

"Excuse me," murmured Ronicky. "I was only joking, and if —"

"Why not?" she exclaimed, more to herself than to him.

Then, to their astonishment, she pushed the paper into the hand of Ronicky and opened the Bible.

"Read the first group!" she commanded.

"One, one, three, two," said Ronicky obediently.

"Book one. That's Genesis. Chapter one, third verse, second word — 'God.' Ronicky, perhaps we have it, but I mistrust that beginning. People don't begin codes with the word God. But no! What he'd use would be merely the first letter of the word. That must be it. The first letter is G. Next?"

"One, one, six, five," read Ronicky dutifully, but his voice was uneven with his excitement.

"Book one, chapter one, sixth verse, fifth word!" translated Jerry Dawn. "And the word is 'there.' Oh, Ronicky, we're lost! There isn't a word in the English language that begins with Gt. But go on."

"One, one, nine, one. And don't give up. We're on the track of something!"

Hugh Dawn said nothing. He sat on a rock with

84

his head buried in his hands, hardly able to endure the tension.

"Ninth verse, first word, 'A.' Gta. Ronicky, we're lost, indeed. That isn't the beginning of any word!"

"Wait a minute," urged Ronicky, as she closed the book with a slam. "Count off the letters in the verses instead of the words. First book, first chapter, third verse, second letter. What does that give you?"

"N."

"Now sixth verse and fifth letter."

"O."

"Ninth verse and first letter."

"A."

"Twelfth verse and fifth letter."

"H. It spells N-O-A-H! Ronicky, we have it!"

A groan of happiness came from Hugh Dawn, who rose and came stumbling to them. Steadily the spelling went on, Ronicky, scribbling down the letters as fast as the girl located them.

In conclusion he read:

Noah and the crescent in line with ravenhead and the vixen twenty down.

"Noah and the crescent in line with ravenhead and the vixen twenty down," repeated Hugh Dawn sourly. "And what the devil good does all the work do when it only brings us to this? Noah and the crescent — twenty down!"

He groaned again.

"Just a minute more," said his daughter, more eagerly than ever. "Doesn't it strike you that those words are like names of places? Noah may be the name of a town. Then 'The Crescent,' and 'Ravenhead,' and 'The Vixen.' "

"But what good do four jumbled names do us?" asked the father.

"I have it!" cried Ronicky. "It's sure plain now that it's down in black and white. Get Noah and The Crescent in line, and then get The Vixen and Ravenhead in line. And at the point where the lines cross, dig down twenty feet!"

Both father and daughter shouted as the whole riddle became clear.

"Heaven bless that iron box!" cried Hugh Dawn.

"And the hammer that busted it!" Ronicky supplemented.

"We're rich," went on Hugh Dawn. "The money's as good as ours. We can start planning how to spend twenty millions. Don't I know the old Ravenhead Mountain? And don't I know The Crescent? And maybe they's a couple of smaller mountains around them parts that are called The Vixen and Mount Noah. I dunno. But we'll start right now for old Ravenhead Mountain!"

# CHAPTER X

## DISASTER

In that determination, however, he was ruled down by Ronicky and Jerry Dawn. For now the twilight was deepening, and the way toward Ravenhead, over rough trails and twenty miles away, according to Dawn's recollection, would make bitter work in the darkness. It was determined, therefore, to wait until the morning. With the first gray of dawn they would start, and by that light they should easily manage to get over the trail to Ravenhead by mid-morning.

Ronicky Doone estimated the time at their disposal.

"We ought," he said, "to have the stuff located by to-morrow night, and while we're working Jerry can ride over the hills and get a wagon and a team of hosses from the nearest town. We'll load and start straight back, and when we get near civilization we can hire enough gents to hold off Moon and his three."

"His three?" Hugh Dawn groaned. "His thirty, more like! He's got 'em scattered through the country, son, and he has ways of getting in touch with 'em pronto. If he got excited about this trail, he might have the whole crowd out combing the country for me inside of twenty-four hours. Still, I think we got time. He'll spend most of to-day hunting by himself. To-night he'll send out his call. Tomorrow they'll spend getting together. And day after tomorrow in the morning he'll be ready to send out his search parties. I've seen him work that way before. But when he sends 'em out, we'll already be snaking south for the railroad, hit it, and slide off east! Ronicky, for the first time in his life Moon is going to be beat! Not a chance in a million that he'll ever connect me up with the old Cosslett treasure. Not a chance that he'll think I'm hunting for it. He'll figure me to be lying out in the hills waiting for a few days. And he'll comb the country around Trainor before he steps out farther."

The matter was allowed to rest there. Before the shack of Cosslett they built a fire of the wood which had been torn from the little veranda floor, and there they cooked their evening meal.

It was dark before they had ended. Afterward they went inside the shack. It was possible to clear the bunk and prop up its broken side after removing the fallen rafter. That made a comfortable bed for the girl. As for Ronicky and Hugh Dawn, they would sleep on the floor.

In the meantime, after putting down their blankets, Ronicky declared his intention of taking a ride on Lou by way of a nightcap. For he declared that he could not possibly sleep so soon after their rest of the midday. Father and daughter had too much to talk over to object strenuously. And a moment later he left the cabin. They heard his mare whinny a greeting to him, and then the roll of her gallop passed down the hill and out of hearing. Hugh Dawn listened to the disappearing sound, his head cocked upon one side.

"There," he said, "goes a queer one!"

"Queer?" echoed Jerry, with a distinct lack of enthusiasm.

"That's what I said. Never saw the like of him yet, and I've seen a pile of men, rough and smooth and all kinds."

"Of all the kinds I've known," said his daughter hotly, "he's the finest, the bravest, the most generous."

"Sure, sure! He's all of that and more. I'm not holding it against him. But he's a wild one, if ever I saw a man!"

"Wild?"

"What d'you call it when a fellow hears news about somebody he's never heard mentioned before, and then rides twenty miles and takes his life in his hands to give a warning?"

"You haven't told me yet — so many things have been happening — how you came to catch him in the hall of the house."

"I was at the window in the hall. I saw Ronicky climb up the side of the house, but the distance and the dark made it a hard job to shoot from where I was, even though I was sure that he was one of Moon's men come for me. I sneaked around into the place in front of the stairs where they turn into the hall on the second floor, and when he came down I flashed the electric torch at him and shot. How I missed, I don't know. But he changed into a wild cat the minute the light hit him. He jumped here and there like a flash, and before I could land him he swung on me and knocked me out. Where he got the muscle to do it out of those skinny arms of his, beats me; but it ain't the only thing about him that beats me. Look at the way he talks to his hoss like she was human. Look at the way he goes off riding alone by night!"

"I can understand everything you mention," replied his daughter.

"Sure you can," and Hugh Dawn grinned. "That's because he's smiled at you a couple of times today."

"Do you mean to infer —" began Jerry.

"Don't be proud," chuckled her father.

"I never heard of anything so absurd," said Jerry indignantly. "Why, I — I don't know the man! He's a stranger!"

"Sure. That's why you're blushing like this. You are your mother all over again, my dear, and she was always forming quick likes and dislikes. Heaven bless her! But me, I take more time to think things and folks over. You'll find out that it pays, Jerry, in the long run."

"I don't know what all the talk's about," said the girl a trifle uneasily. "If you think that I've been forward with Mr. Doone —"

"There you go!" Her father laughed as he spoke.

90

"I will ask you to stop climbing mountains, and you jump over a cliff instead. I don't mean nothing, except for you to watch your ways with Ronicky. You ain't an ordinary girl, Jerry, dear. You got more looks than most. Not that you're the most beautiful I ever seen, but you got a downright pleasing way, and when you smile your whole face lights up a lot."

"Of course all this is absurd," said Jerry. "But if I choose to be courteous to a man who saved your life — both our lives, perhaps — is there anything wrong in it?"

"Courtesy is one thing; it ain't what I'm talking about," said her father gravely.

"And the other thing?"

"Well, Jerry, I'd a pile rather see you dead than get seriously interested in a gent like Ronicky Doone."

She stared at him, almost frightened.

"I see," said he, very grave, "that you've been thinking even more than I suspected."

"Dad," she cried, "this is insufferable. Oblique expressions like these only serve to —"

"Tie them big words up, brand 'em, and keep 'em for the fancy markets," said her father gruffly. "I don't foller 'em easy. Talk plain. I'm a plain man. And I tell you plainly that I love you too much to see you throw away time on one like Doone. For why? Because he's a will-o'-the-wisp, my dear. He's one of these gents who go through life without ever settling down to one thing. He's about what? Twenty-five, I'd take him to be. Well,

Jerry, he's crammed ten times more fighting inside his twenty-five years than I've put inside forty-five. A fighting man is like a fighting wolf — they'd better hunt alone!"

"You don't mean," she said, "that he's a gun fighter!"

"Don't I? Well, honey, you got to learn to use your eyes! What does it mean when a gent carries his holster slung away down low on his right hip so's it's just within twitching distance of his finger tips? Ain't that to have it ready for a fast draw? And what does it mean when a gent's left hand is all pale from being in a glove, and when his right hand is brown as a berry?"

"Because the left hand is the bridle hand."

"Because the right hand is the gun hand, Jerry!"

She winced at his surety.

"I'm as sure of it," said her father, blowing a great cloud of smoke from his pipe, "as I am that my name is Hugh Dawn. And watch his hands. Long and slender and nervous. No flesh on 'em. He's never made a living by work. No calluses on those hands. Nothing to keep them from being fast as a flash of light — like the hands of a musician, they look to me. Always doing something with that right hand of his. His left hand is used to hanging steady on the reins, and it's always lying still. But his right hand ain't never still. It's always jumping about and rapping on something, or going here and there and everywhere just for the sake of being under way. I'll tell you why: Because that's the right hand that's saved the life of

Ronicky Doone more'n once! It's the hand that's got his trigger finger! It's his fortune!"

"You mean," breathed the girl, "that he's a professional gunman — a murderer?"

"Not a bit! He wouldn't take advantage of his skill with a gun — not to hurt anybody. But I'll wager he's got his man before now. I'll wager that before he dies he'll get a pile more. It's wrote in big letters all over him."

"He'll change," said Jerry Dawn feverishly. "I know that he'll change!"

"Maybe you could do the changing?" said her father.

Her flush was at least a partial admission that she had had the thought.

"Some girls," said he, "are so plumb good that they marry a man for the sake of being close to him and reforming him. Sometimes they do. Ronicky Doone is a fine gent. Brave, honest as the day's long, generous. But he ain't meant for a girl to love. I'm putting it strong. I don't mean that you feel anything like that for him yet. I'm just warning you. Because if you just give a gent like that a kind look, you may set him on fire; he starts making love like a fire in a storm; first thing you know, you're engaged. And that's the end. Jerry, you'll watch out?"

As he leaned earnestly toward her he saw her face whiten, saw her eyes widen. There was a ghost-seeing look about her, and instantly Hugh Dawn knew that a horror was standing in the door of the cabin. Instinctively he measured the distance

93

to his gun. Like a fool he had hung it with his belt on a nail against the wall. It was hopelessly out of arm's length.

He turned his head with a convulsive jerk, and there in the door he saw Jack Moon.

# CHAPTER XI

## THE TRAP

There was no gun in his hand, and yet the man radiated danger. His silent coming, the very smile with which he looked down on them, were filled with terror-inspiring qualities. As for Hugh Dawn, he uttered a faint groan and then whirled out of his chair and stood upon his widely braced feet. Even when Dawn reeled back within reaching distance of his gun on the wall and made a motion toward it, the tall man in the door did not offer to draw his own weapon, but the smile hardened a little on his mouth, and his eyes grew fixed.

Jerry knew that it was Jack Moon. She had never seen his face, never even heard it accurately described; but somehow she knew that the man there in the doorway was the root of all evil.

Suddenly she leaped from the bunk and cast herself before her father. That sudden motion had brought the revolver into the hand of Moon, but it was instantly restored to its holster. The double movement had been merely a flash of light. Such speed of hand was uncanny.

"Steady," said the outlaw. "No cause for jumping in front of the sneak, lady. I ain't going to

95

shoot him right away. Not right away. Maybe never. All depends on how him and me come to agree. Or maybe we'll agree to disagree. Just you sit down yonder where you were, miss. No harm'll come to you." He removed his hat and bowed to her, and in so doing he half turned his back on her father.

She knew that the devilish brain of the man had inspired this maneuver to tempt her father into action. But Hugh Dawn was in no condition to fight. His will was paralyzed. He could not fight any more than the bird can escape from the hypnotic eye of the snake.

"They tell hard tales about Jack Moon," went on the big man, thus announcing himself, "but they never yet whispered a story about him laying a finger on a woman, young or old. I can tell you to lay to it that you're as safe with me as if you was a six-months-old baby in the arms of your mother. It ain't you I aim to talk to — it's that!"

He indicated her father with a jerk of his thumb. But for some reason his contempt did not degrade Hugh Dawn. The man would fight willingly enough against odds which were at all even. But he recognized the madness of a bulldog attacking a lion. Even as great as this was the contrast, it was not that Moon was so much larger in physical dimensions. But he was made bigger by an inward lordliness that overflowed. The poise of his head was that of a conqueror. His spirit towered above her father like the young Achilles over some nameless Trojan warrior.

"I seen the box outside," said Jack Moon. "What was in it, Dawn?"

There was no resistance in Dawn. He pointed sullenly to the slip of paper lying on the bed — the paper on which had been written the directions for reaching the site of the treasure.

The bandit strode across the room and reached for it, but the girl, with a lightning movement, forestalled him. She swept it up, leaped away from Moon, who followed with a startled exclamation, and, balling the paper to a hard knot as she ran, she reached the window above the lake and threw the paper as far as her strength allowed. The wind was blowing in that direction, and the precious slip would be wafted down to the waters of the lake.

The hand of Jack Moon was checked in the very act of falling on her shoulder and turning her around. But when she faced him, white and drawn about the lips, he was smiling again.

"That took nerve," he said, "seeing the reputation I got around these parts. But I got to tell you this, lady: It don't do even for ladies to fool with Jack Moon. I don't handle 'em the way I handle men, but most generally I find ways of makin' 'em behave. Now" — and here he turned on Hugh Dawn — "tell me what was on that paper!"

"No, no," shouted the girl. "Don't you see, dad, that it's the price of your own head?"

"There you are again," said Jack Moon sternly,

seeing that the exclamation had sealed the lips of Dawn as the latter was about to speak. "You'll have to learn better than that, lady, before you're with me long. Dawn, will you open up and tell me?"

The gun gleamed in his hand. He thrust it against the breast of Dawn.

"Now talk quick," he muttered. "I know everything, Dawn. Treat heard you and Whitwell, but I want to get the yarn out of your own mouth. I'll tell you this, Dawn: if you open up, maybe they'll be a way out for you!"

"Don't talk, don't talk!" cried Jerry Dawn. "Don't trust him, dad!"

"If you care for your rotten soul," said Jack Moon, "come out with it, Dawn!"

The latter groaned: "What price d'you pay, Moon?"

"Price? What sort of a price d'you ask?"

"Freedom," said Dawn. "And your word on it."

"Would you trust him?" moaned Jerry.

"Be quiet, Jerry," said her father. "No matter what else Moon is, he's a man of his word. It's never been broke yet."

"But it's seldom given," replied Moon coolly. "Why should I give it to you now?"

"How high," retorted Dawn, "d'you put the price on my life?"

"Prices? I dunno. Prices change. I've known gents I'd shoot as soon as I'd kill a dog. I've known some that would have to pay thousands to buy themselves off. But for a gent that's double crossed me the way you've done — well, it'd have to be high!"

Hugh Dawn nodded.

"How high?" he asked.

"Everything you got," said the outlaw, "would be enough."

To the astonishment of the girl, her father shook his head, puzzled.

"You can make your choice," said Moon. "Either you turn over the whole Cosslett stuff to me or —"

"I haven't got the Cosslett money. You know that!"

"You've got the plan to show where it is."

"Suppose the plan turns out wrong?"

The admission implied in this question made the eyes of Jack Moon blaze.

"By the gods," he whispered, "you did get it!"

"You lied to me, then," growled Dawn. "Treat didn't hear Whitwell talk about the box and what he thought was in it!"

"Treat didn't hear anything. But now that I know you've got the plan inside your head, come out with it, Dawn, and you and me will make a dicker. Wait! Here's something that the rest of the boys have got to vote on. You can thank your stars that I've got the majority of the crew with me!"

He whistled, a shrill, fluting sound long prolonged, and there was a rushing of horses' hoofs up the slope to the crest of the hill. Presently the door and the windows were packed with ominous faces, and there was everywhere the glittering of drawn guns. Nearly a dozen men had gathered around the little ruined shanty in the space of a few seconds. Well indeed had it been for Hugh Dawn that he had not attacked the leader when the latter was seemingly alone.

"Boys," said Jack Moon to the dark faces which waited silently, all turned toward Dawn and his daughter, "I've run him down, but it seems that he can offer a price. I want to know what figure you'd put on his head?"

"Whitwell was my pal," said a voice sternly. "What price was he given a chance to pay? I say shoot the skunk and have it done with."

Another voice growled: "What price was Gandil given a chance to pay? Wasn't he a better man than Dawn ever dreamed of being? I say shoot the skunk!"

"Wait a minute, boys"' said the leader, raising his hand. "You got as good a right to vote on this as I have. And you're going to have your way. You know I always see to that. But first I want you to know the whole facts. The price that Dawn can pay is the whole Cosslett treasure."

That astonishing news brought a gasp from every member of the band. Evidently Moon had talked about that accumulation of wealth enough to have filled the fancies of his wild followers.

"Are you sure of that?" asked a number of voices.

"I'm sure he's got the plan."

"And if we don't find the stuff?"

"Then Dawn dies. That's easy, ain't it? We give him our word that if we get the gold, he goes scot-free. If we don't get it, he dies. Are you with me, boys?"

"How much," said another voice, "d'you figure that gold would come to?"

"Five millions at least, and maybe anything up to twenty. Hard to believe all the yarns they told about that gold. Sometimes they got so excited they multiplied everything by four. Sometimes they got so careless about gold, and so used to it, that they understated things. I dunno how the Cosslett treasure stands, but I figure on five millions as the least we'd get. Think it over, boys! You and me! altogether, make fourteen. Add three more shares for me, which is only my right, and that makes seventeen. Seventeen into five million — how much does that make? Close to three hundred thousand dollars apiece, lads. Close to three hundred thousand! Put that out at seven per cent. That gives you twenty thousand a year. Think it over! That's the price that Hugh Dawn can offer for his life. The biggest haul that was ever made in the mountains. Twenty thousand dollars to every one of you every year of your lives. Is it worth his life to you, boys?"

There was a moment of bewildered silence, and then a mutter of astonishment. Those eyes were calculating, spending, already.

"Cut all that down by one third," said Hugh Dawn suddenly. "I've just thought of something."

Moon turned on him with a snarl of anger.

"Are you going to bargain with me about it?" he asked. "Ain't you satisfied with having your ratty life?"

For the first time Hugh Dawn did not shrink. He met the eye of Jack Moon steadily.

"Tell you how it is," he said. "I can buy you off with my share of the stuff, and Jerry's share. But she and me ain't the only ones. They's another gent that has to be figured in. 'Twasn't for him we'd never be here. It was him that warned me you was coming, him that got us safely up here, and him that helped us work out the puzzle. Moon, you got nothin' agin' him, and he's got to come in for a third of everything you get! Understand?"

The girl was amazed. Her heart had been sinking, her blood growing cold, in the feeling that her father had from first to last in this encounter played the part of a coward. This sudden defiance of Jack Moon bewildered her. Then she began to make out the reasons for it. It was not the actual danger that terrified her father; he was simply paralyzed by the name and the presence of Moon. The outlaw was as amazed as any one could have been by this resistance, and by the revelation of these secrets.

"The gent that warned you?" he echoed. "Warned you I was coming?"

"He heard everything. He was in the barn. He rode around you and got to me and fought his way into the house to tell me you was coming."

"I got a lot to thank this gent for," said the leader calmly. "Him and me ought to be able to come to an understanding. What's his name?"

"Ronicky Doone, he called himself. And he's sure a square shooter."

"Ronicky Doone?" echoed the outlaw. "Well, I'll pass the word to the boys that if a gent shows up pretty soon, they're not to take a pot shot at him. They got a habit of using up ammunition plumb careless that way. Si!"

Treat strode through the door.

"You remember how Dawn plugged you through the leg? Now you stay here and watch him, Si, and see he don't get loose from you. Understand?"

The teeth of Treat showed through the tangles of his black beard and mustache. Calmly he drew his revolver and sat down with the weapon balanced on his knee and pointing toward Hugh Dawn.

The leader left the shack and with a gesture gathered half a dozen of his men around him.

"Baldy, you take charge. Take these gents along with you. Post 'em scattering out along the hillside so's to cover every direction. You heard the name of the gent that's up here along with Hugh?"

"Nope."

"Ronicky Doone! Ever hear of him?"

"Seems like I have, sort of in patches, somewhere."

"If you'd ever been down South you'd of heard a pile more than patches about him. He's the most nacheral gun fighter that ever drilled a gent full of lead. Baldy, go out on the hill and watch. Don't shoot till you get him close. And then don't ask no questions. Just blaze away. I'm going back inside and tell 'em that I've arranged for a nice quiet reception for Doone. When you've dropped him, I'll go busting out and raise the devil, like I'd give you strict orders not to do any shooting. Understand?"

Baldy whispered an assent.

"If you want to have something to give you a grudge agin' him, I can tell you that this is the gent that overheard us in the barn, and that rode ahead and warned Dawn we was coming. Now scatter out yonder, and mind you shoot low."

# CHAPTER XII

## BARGAIN

"We'll go on with the dicker," explained Jack Moon, returning to the cabin, "as soon as this Doone comes along. We'll settle down all nice and peaceable and get to an agreement like friends. Which there ain't any reason why we shouldn't be friends, Dawn; and so far as you're concerned, I don't see no reason why I couldn't fix you up with one of my shares of the stuff before we're through."

Jerry studied the man with the most intense curiosity. Certainly he was a person of varying moods. Now, when he talked again, she noted that he paid more and more attention to her and less and less to her father, as though he recognized in her a force which had to be reckoned with. According to his explanation, everything would work out smoothly. As soon as Ronicky Doone approached, they would sit down and come to an understanding. He had already sent out his men, he said, to watch for the coming of Doone, and he would be brought in to share the discussion on equal terms. It might be difficult to induce his men, he said, to consent to so large a share as one third going to Doone. But no doubt they could compromise handsomely, and every one would be satisfied.

Yet, while he talked, she branded every one of his words as a lie. Not that she hated him. There was a mixture of respect with the fear with which she regarded him, and where respect enters in, there is never a complete detestation. But it was respect for his cool prowess rather than for his moral qualities. What gave her the chief doubt was that he, having so manifestly the upper hand, should be so carefully considerate of others as he was pretending to be of Dawn, herself, and the absent Ronicky Doone. How greatly would the whole problem of the division be simplified, for instance, if a bullet should strike down Ronicky Doone!

No sooner had the idea occurred to her than she was reasonably sure that it had occurred to the bandit also, and she began to strain her ear painfully for the first sound of the sand and gravel under the hoofs of the approaching Lou. In the meantime, Hugh Dawn had recovered his mental poise to a large degree, and when the leader spoke to him, he was able to answer calmly. He even entered into some details of his experiences in the East since he left Trainor, and told of the hard work which had enabled him to make enough money to support his girl from the distance and send her to school.

"But what beats me," said Jack Moon, "is that you didn't send for her. Why not, Hugh?"

"Because," said the other quietly, "I knew

pretty well that you were watching her close all the time, and that the minute she made a move out of the country you'd follow her on the chance that she might be trying to get to see me. If I sent for her, I'd be doing the same thing as sending for you."

Jack Moon shook his head.

"You see," he complained to the girl, "they's some folks that never get over being suspicious. Follow a girl trying to get back to her father? I leave it to you, Miss Dawn, if I look to be that sort of a —"

Here she lost track of his words, because far off she heard the hoofs of a horse crunching into the gravel at the bottom of the hill on which Cosslett's shack stood. The horse came at a steady and swinging gallop. The picture of Ronicky Doone on the lively mare rushed into her mind. Suddenly she started to her feet and shouted: "Ronicky! Danger!"

Far away through the night thrilled her voice. Before an echo could pick it up, there was the crash of half a dozen firearms. Then came the rushing of the galloping horse withdrawing, and last of all a far-flung yell of defiance. Ronicky Doone had escaped.

The girl turned from the window.

"Is this the square deal you'd planned for Ronicky Doone?" she asked fiercely. "Is this what you did? Ah, I read your mind all the while."

The bandit was shaking his head as though bewildered.

"How come all this, I dunno. Maybe when Doone heard you yell he fired, and my boys answered him. That's human nature, and you can't blame them for doing it, I guess. Eh?"

She smiled scornfully.

"Treat!" called the leader.

When the black-bearded man entered, Jack Moon left the cabin hastily. "I'll make out if the fools have done any harm to him," he called back to Jerry Dawn.

Once outside, however, he broke into a run, cursing under his breath, and so came to the group of Baldy's men making slowly back toward the cabin. Jack Moon plunged through their midst until he came to his lieutenant, whose shoulder he gripped with fingers of iron.

"Curse you for a fool!" he said bitterly. "I told you to hold your fire till you were sure of him!"

"Then why didn't you keep that she-devil from screeching? He was about in point-blank range. I was all ready to give the signal, and then she yelled, and he turned."

"Did you drill him at all?"

"What chance did I have in this light? Even the stars are dim. And he started his hoss swerving. No more chance of dropping him than there was of killing a cloud shadow. He was gone, and that was all there was to it."

Jack Moon cursed again, and without further speech he turned on his heel and strode back for the cabin.

But he was smiling again when he got to the place.

"Just as I figured," he said. "When you yelled you scared Doone into pulling his gun and shooting at the first shadow he saw, and my boys figured he was shooting at them, so they gave him a volley. That was all they was to it. But he got off without being hurt." He went on soberly: "But this messes things up. Most likely this Ronicky Doone will send back for help to get you folks free. That being the case, we got not a ghost of a chance to get to the treasure. He knows the secret, and he'll lead all the men he can raise straight to the spot and keep me off; and that, Dawn, makes it pretty hard on you, I'd say — pretty hard!"

His eyes bored cruelly into the eyes of his intended victim.

"There goes your price that you was going to pay," he continued. "There it goes up in smoke. Before morning Doone will have fifty men headed for the place!"

Hugh Dawn raised a hand.

"Gimme one minute alone with you," he urged.

The leader assented, and Dawn stepped out of the door and into the darkness.

"You don't need to have no fear of Doone," he said, as soon as they were safely out of earshot of the girl. "He knows that I ain't much more of a friend to the law than you are. He knows that I can't have a sheriff asking me questions. He knows, besides, that I was a member of your crowd once."

"You think, for your sake, he'll let five million dollars go?"

"I don't think. I know," replied the other. "That's the kind of a gent he is. Not ordinary by no means, Moon."

"What d'you figure on doing now? What am I to do? Take a chance that this man-killing Doone, that I've heard about, won't call in a crowd to clean up on me? From what I've heard about him, Dawn, he'd rather find a fight than a million, and when he gets a chance for fighting and money at the same time, why, he'll just start and run amuck. I'm talking to you straight, son, because I dunno how to figure. You know him, and I don't."

"I'll tell you this," said Hugh Dawn, knowing that in spite of the quiet of Moon, the subject up for discussion was whether or not he, Dawn, should be killed and left or whether the outlaw should bargain his life against his secret. "I'll tell you this: Ronicky Doone won't make a move to get help, because he knows that the minute he shows up with a crowd behind him, the first thing you'll do will be to plug me."

"Is he as fond of you as all that?"

"Moon, this gent Doone is a killer. I guess you know that already, but if you don't know it, I'll tell you. But besides being a killer, he's as square a shooter as ever I seen! He shook hands to go through this game with me, and he'll go through thinking just as much of my skin as if it was his own. You can lay to that positive. I know!"

There was something entirely convincing about

his manner of speaking. And indeed he was one of the few men in the world whom Moon was willing to believe, at least in part. He stood somewhat in awe of the honesty of Hugh Dawn. This was the only man that had ever come into his clutches and escaped unstained by grim crimes. There was not another man in his band at the present moment that had not committed at least one murder or participated in a killing. Dawn alone had withdrawn from the horrible necessity of obeying the leader, even though he knew that that withdrawal drew down the vengeance of the band on his head.

"Hugh," he said at last. "I'm going to take the chance. The stake's large enough to make it worth while. Tell me the secret you learned out of the box, and I'll give you my word and my hand, before we take another step, that no harm shall come to you from me. Will you do that?"

"And Doone?" insisted Hugh Dawn stubbornly.

"Doone's share? The best I can promise is that I'll get the boys to vote him as much as I can. Will that do?"

"It'll have to," admitted Hugh Dawn. "And here's my hand, Jack."

# CHAPTER XIII

## TRAILING

The whisper of bullets about his head, as he whirled his mare down the slope of the hill, had given Ronicky Doone a veritable volume of explanations. The number of the guns and the girl's shrill cry of warning to which he owed his safety, were ample testimony that Jack Moon and his band had reached the cabin and captured the father and daughter.

But had they spared the girl and killed the man, as it seemed that their most logical course of action would dictate? That problem filled the mind of Ronicky as he scurried away to the safety of the trees and the darkness. And it stayed with him during the long vigil of the night.

If Hugh Dawn were dead, then the great necessity was to gather other men at once and free the girl from Moon's band. But if there had been a chance for talk, it stood to reason that they could bargain with Moon, the treasure against their lives. If he rashly brought on a posse to free the prisoners, it also stood to reason that Moon would kill Hugh Dawn before he fled from the power of the law.

He reviewed the case, in fact, exactly as Hugh Dawn had prophesied he would. The best conclusion to which he could come was that he had better linger on the outskirts on the march of the outlaws and do them what damage he could until he had reduced their numbers, or until he found an opportunity of making a dash to win the freedom of the girl and her father in case both were alive. What he chiefly worried about was the man, for he knew Westerners and their ways well enough to understand that a girl need have no fear, so long as she was in their midst. The most they would do would be to keep the pair for some time in their company until they had reached a far portion of the mountains, and then they would send her back. But even on the point of their treatment of the girl he could not be sure, for his memory of the pale, handsome face of Jack Moon brought up the most evil forebodings. The man must be capable of any crime.

With these thoughts to disturb him, Ronicky passed a miserable night, and in the first gray of the dawn he made out, from the shack on the hill beside Cunningham Lake, the signs of preparations for breakfast.

His own meal consisted of hard-tack, while Lou grazed in a meadow of rich grass which he had found behind the outskirts of the trees.

The meal on the cliff was followed by saddling and mounting, and now Ronicky strained his eyes from the covert of the trees as he had never strained them before.

He could not distinguish faces. But he made out the form of the girl on her gray horse, placed about halfway down the long procession, and beside her rode another figure on another gray horse. It must be her father.

He waited, however, until the whole cavalcade had moved on. There were now fourteen men besides the girl and her father; evidently the whole Moon band had assembled at the Cosslett cabin during the night. The thirteen were led by one so formidable as Jack Moon. It was indeed a Herculean task even to dream of thwarting so many practiced fighters. And yet the eyes of Ronicky Doone gleamed with evil desire, and he caressed the butt of his rifle. Rapid fire might greatly reduce that company, but at the first shot he knew another bullet would be driven into the body of Hugh Dawn.

He dismissed all shadow of doubt as to whether or not Hugh Dawn lived by climbing into the saddle on Lou and riding to the cabin. There he made a careful search for crimson stains, and, finding none, he was certain that there had been no death in Cosslett's shack.

It needed a long detour to the left to come in sight of the riders again. He picked them up in the midst of a difficult trail, almost blind, that ran among the mountains north and west. The direction made the heart of Ronicky leap, for it convinced him that Jack Moon had at length learned the secret of the treasure. The bargain had indeed been made!

After that Ronicky hung less closely on the heels of the riders. It was a needless courting of danger, and if the distance to the burial place were twenty miles, as Dawn had estimated, he need not dog their footsteps every inch of the way.

He contented himself with coming into view only occasionally, weaving from one side of the trail to the other so that, in case he had been seen and a small rear party were detached to take him, he would not be located in the expected place. But always, when he had a chance to count the numbers of the procession, the original fifteen came to view.

It was mid-morning when they debouched out of the upper mountains into a steep-sided hollow. To the southeast a narrow, deep ravine carried out into the distance the waters of a little creek which flashed with arrowy swiftness from among the pines of the northern slope. Wood, water, a shelter from the winds — what more could man wish for a camping ground? The existence of the trail across the mountains was readily explained by the pitted sides of the hollow. There had been mines here, many a year before, and the trail had been worn by the hundreds of pack mules and horses; rocks had been cleared away here, trees hewn down there.

Ronicky was in time to see the procession turn into a mad rush for the bottom of the hollow as soon as the crest was topped. Helter-skelter down the side they rushed, and in the bottom land below he saw them dancing like mad creatures as they flung themselves from their horses. Only the two figures on the grays retained their saddles. The rest seemed to be intoxicated, and no doubt this was the gold-madness taking hold of them.

After the first frenzy they were seen to be swirling around a central, commanding figure seated on a bay horse of unusual size, and Ronicky did not need a field glass to pick the man out as Jack Moon. For this was the directing mind which presently sent men scrambling here and there. He himself joined the workers, and after a time Ronicky could make out that they were lining up two tall mountains to the north and crossing this line with another drawn through two other peaks in the east.

If he had doubted before, this work convinced him that he was right. Yonder sway-backed mountain to the east — that was unquestionably The Crescent. After a time, on the far side of a little mound in the hollow, three shovels and as many picks began to flash rhythmically and swiftly. The task of digging had commenced.

Most of the party remained here. But Jack Moon, the Dawns, and two more men rode up the course of the creek and disappeared under the pines, obviously in search of a good camping place. Ronicky turned Lou to the left and cut around the hollow to make out what luck they had.

He left Lou a short distance back in the woods, after he had come reasonably close to the course of the brook, and went out cautiously on foot. It was not hard to skulk safely through the forest, since there was a dense growth of virgin wood in many places, and, in others, thickets even more favorable to secret approaches. So he came to an opening in the woods and found there the whole party which had climbed from the hollow. He was quite near — not more than a hundred yards away, perhaps; and he made out the face of Hugh Dawn for the first time, standing beside Jack Moon.

Around them spread five little shanties which in the days of the mines had been put up by the laborers close together for the sake of sharing the advantages of the natural clearing and enjoying one another's company. Time had not completely ruined the little buildings, for they were of logs, rudely squared to be sure, but put together solidly enough to stand another generation, perhaps. The two men of Moon's band who had joined the party of exploration were already busy clearing some fallen logs to the entrance of one of the huts.

This was as much as Ronicky desired to learn. Before late afternoon the hut would be occupied, the horses picketed in the rich surrounding meadow, and the whole band quartered at ease. Ronicky could not but admire such faultless system as this. The chances were that they would be able to get down to the treasure by the digging of a single day. But if they did not, here he was equipped with a flawless camp. It was a part of good generalship.

With this much ascertained, Ronicky started back to find Lou and locate some close quarters of his own in the near distance.

# CHAPTER XIV

## THE FIRST ATTEMPT

The hole was deepening rapidly. The few hours of work had brought about amazing results, for the ground in this place was a loose mixture of sand and gravel; without using picks to loosen it first, the men simply shoveled as fast as their arms and backs could swing. They had made the first cut amply wide, and now, narrowing the pit at the depth of twelve feet, they left a ledge onto which the diggers cast up the dirt while two men on the shelf tossed it up again in relay to a great heap which was growing on the lip of the cut. They were down sixteen feet, and who could tell when a thrusting shovel might strike the treasure? So they were working like mad, never speaking, never even pausing to wipe the dropping sweat from their faces. Only the occasional grunt of effort rolled up, hollow and dull-sounding, from the deep hole.

"Go up the hill and bring Dawn and his girl," said the chief. "Ought to be getting close to twenty feet now, and I want 'em to see as much as we see."

Accordingly, a messenger hurried up the course

of the creek to the hut and returned to Dawn and the girl. In the meantime, the men had been arranged in four shifts by the leader. Three men were always on guard, overlooking the hole and at the cabins. Three more dug in the pit, and six were kept in reserve. Every half hour the shifts changed. The workers from the pit went up to stand their guard. The guard came back to wait for a turn in the pit, and three fresh men jumped down to take the shovels whose handles were kept warm from the friction of labor.

Meanwhile Dawn and Jerry arrived.

A tape was now run down the side of the pit, and a shout of exultation announced that they had cut a full nineteen feet. They gathered in a rush around the edges of the hole, so close, indeed, that the lip of the pit caved under one man and precipitated him, tumbling and yelling, to the bottom. But he came to his feet, snatched the shovel from the hands of a tired worker, and himself assailed the bottom-ground with fury.

The dirt came up in a steady shower now, and there was no sound but the ringing scrape of little stones on the thin metal of the shovel blades as the gravel was flung high. The watchers swayed and stooped in harmony with the workers, as though by joining the rhythm they were joining the labor and helping. Now the tape measured twenty feet at the edges of the hole. In the center it reached to twenty-one.

The laborers paused. Of one accord they raised their gloomy faces to the watchers above. Then,

119

with not a word said by those above or those below, the task began again. Two more feet the hole was sunk. And then, uncalled, the men in the pit clambered to the surface, bringing their tools with them.

Solid silence continued. The digging of the hole had brought the thought of the golden hoard close to every one. For an hour, every time a worker had thrust in his shovel and turned the edge against a solid rock, he had jerked it out expecting to find the tip bright with glittering yellow. At length:

"We must of made wrong measurements," said Moon. "We sure must of got the mountains lined up wrong, boys!"

No one else ventured to answer until Silas Treat spoke.

"Jack," he said, "I looked over those sightings. I got 'em lined up proper. There's The Vixen; there's The Crescent, and the point at the left is the peak of The Crescent. There's Mount Noah, and there's The Ravenhead. Don't I know this country like I was born and raised here? No, sir, we sure got the right peaks lined up, and we sunk the old hole more'n twenty feet. Jack, they simply ain't no treasure here, and old Cosslett, cuss his white-livered hulk, had a laugh at us while he was dying! Wish I had him here now, so I could plug him once more myself."

Afterward, Jerry Dawn wondered why that brutal speech did not shock her. But at the time she was intent on only one interest — gold! She paid no attention to even the surly faces around her.

Here was a problem, and the reward for solving it was thousands of pounds of solid gold. She could not doubt that the treasure was buried in this vicinity. The slip of paper and the figures on it had been real; the code could not have lied to her.

"But suppose," she said at length, "that Cosslett didn't know this country as well as you, Mr. Treat. To him it might be impossible to calculate which tip of The Crescent is the highest. It lies there like a new moon, on its back. Suppose he took the other tip as his guide and lined it up with Mount Noah beyond. That would bring the line farther over to our right."

She began walking, climbed a little mound, and stood on the top of it, shading her eyes and peering under the flat of her hand.

"Here's where the line would fall, Mr. Treat. And surely the chance is worth trying. I know we can't fail."

The black look with which Jack Moon had been regarding Hugh Dawn cleared a little.

"Boys," he said, "shall we try it? Not now, because we've done a day's work already, and night's almost here. But to-morrow?"

The expectant face of the girl had produced the inevitable reaction. The gold fever, which had exhausted them with the first great disappointment, returned with new force. There was but one gloomy voice of foreboding.

"Here's the place, right enough," said Silas Treat, following the girl and, like her, squinting to line Mount Noah with the south crest of The

Crescent, "but look here. How come old Cosslett was so strong he could bury his gold under rocks like this one?"

He pointed to a great boulder on which he was standing. He leaned and laid hold on a ragged projecting edge. The rock did not move.

"Cosslett wasn't never the man I am," he declared. "If I can't budge this rock, how come it that old Cosslett could ever have put stones like this in the way?"

"He might have had other men working for him," answered Jack Moon. "That ain't hard to explain."

"Hire gents? Gents that would know where the gold was buried as well as he knew? That don't sound like Cosslett! He always played it safe!"

"Maybe when the hole was dug he just up and plugged 'em and buried 'em on top of the money," suggested Jack Moon. "That sounds reasonable."

"Maybe it's got a reasonable sound to you," Silas Treat returned gruffly, "but it's got a devilish bad sound to me. Anyway, if you want to dig, I'll bear a hand. Only, how come these big rocks here?"

Jerry Dawn pointed up the nearest side of the hollow.

"See where the trees have been torn away along the hill by a landslide?" she exclaimed. "That same landslide must have rolled these rocks down. It made the mound, too. And we'll have to dig through the mound and then twenty feet beneath it. But I know that the gold is here! I feel it!"

"That's what all green hands at prospecting talk

122

like," declared one of the men.

"The girl's talking sense, though," retorted another. "More sense than ever come out of your head, Nick! We'll make that try, Jack!"

"Good!" the leader said.

# CHAPTER XV

## MOTIVES AND MEN

The dirt began to crash back into the hole as Jerry
Dawn turned away and looked upon the ending
of the strangest day of her life. All the forested
sides of the evergreen hollow were gilded now with
sunset colors falling on the trees, crimsons and
golds of exquisite dimness, pastel shades almost
too faint for the most exact eye. Beyond, the
greater mountaintops walked up to the brighter
color of the horizon sky, and to the zenith was
an infinite reach of the eye — the purity of blue
distance.

The girl drew close to her father with a chas-
tened heart. Looking into his seamed, sorrow-
worn face, she was able to understand those wild
moments of his younger life which now placed him
in peril. She was able to forgive the cruelty of
carelessness and neglect which had broken the
heart of her mother. For the big man was only
a product of this big country — intense in passions,
big of will, great of heart, and sublime in indif-
ference.

Such men are needed to mate the Western
mountains, she thought. If she were able to extend

her influence around him, how vitally he might be changed, and in how short a time! His had been too muscular a nature to submit to life and gain lessons from it in his youth. The milder hours of receptivity were reserved for his maturer years. She looked on him with a touch of pity, a hallowed emotion; she looked on him as she might have looked on a child.

His face, also, had been raised as he followed her glance to the central sky. But when he looked down to her he murmured: "Well, Jerry, here's another day ending, and I'm still alive!"

She only took his hand in both of hers and gripped it hard. Her finger tips closed over deep, stiff calluses. However wild he might once have been, he had proved his worth by the bitter labor which earned money enough to give her a schooling. Through her mind flashed in swift procession, memories of the letters which had come to her from the East, never with an address to guide her answer, for fear that that address might become known to Jack Moon.

Each letter had contained a money order; and about each money order was always wrapped a bit of paper over which, in a sprawling, stiff hand, were traced a few formal words. Their formality she had not been able to understand until she grew much older. And then she knew that it is typical of the uneducated. The written word is to them a fearsome thing. Their thoughts come forth haltingly on paper. They blush at attempted tenderness. They feel that they are addressing the world, and therefore they write to their nearest and dearest as though they were writing to strangers.

She was still thinking of these things when she heard the deep and musical voice of Jack Moon behind her. It was a voice rare indeed! It might have been used to move thousands of men. And always when the man spoke she was conscious of the strong mind, the strong will behind the words. There was ever something about Jack Moon as strong as his muscles, as big as his body. Beyond the power of the flesh there was a secondary power of the spirit. The longer she saw him, the more she knew of him, the greater seemed the extent of the undiscovered bourn behind his eyes.

He was giving his orders for the night, and he issued them with a military precision. To some he gave the task of collecting wood for the big camp fire which was to be built in the central space among the huts. Others still would care for the unpacking. A third crew would do the cooking. And finally the fourth would relieve the two watchers in the forest, who were keeping ward against Ronicky Doone, and would call them toward the cabins, where a fresh guard must be mounted all night to keep off the expected marauder.

With this accomplished, the bandit leader overtook Hugh Dawn and his daughter.

"You, Dawn," he said gruffly; "maybe you think you got a free ticket to chuck and bed and everything, eh? Not a hope of that, son! You mosey along and do your share. You can help the boys

126

with the unpacking. Treat will give you orders just what to do. And mind that you keep in sight. No trying to run off through the trees. Treat has a terrible nervous trigger finger. Now off with you! Go tell Treat that I sent you!"

Hugh Dawn cast a glance at his daughter and then departed.

"And now," said Moon, his voice changed adroitly to fit her hearing, "I got a chance to talk to you private. I been wanting to all day, but one thing or another kept coming up. What I got to say is this: Me and the boys all like you fine, and we aim to give you as good a time as we can, considering everything."

She turned a little and looked him squarely in the eye, smiling whimsically.

"I suppose," said Jack Moon, grave before her subdued mirth, "that that sounds pretty queer to you. I suppose that you got us all wrote down as maneaters that do a couple of murders before breakfast to work up an appetite. That it?"

She examined him somewhat cautiously. She had always thought that the fellow was far too intelligent to have any illusions about himself or about what others might think of him. Now, searching for a trace of stupidity or of weak conceit, she was unable to find it. She saw a noble cast of features, strange only in their unvarying pallor. She had heard of men like this before, whose skins were apparently impervious to the burning rays of the mountain suns, but Moon was the first she had seen.

Aside from his complexion, however, there was nothing curious about his make-up. The mouth was generously large, and formed with a promise of sensitiveness. The chin was cut in a manner to suggest plenty of solid bone beneath. The nose was straight, large enough to give dominance to his face, but perfectly formed. The eyes were large and well separated, and they looked straight as the flight of an arrow. The forehead above was magnificently high and broad, and crowning all was a luxuriant mass of chestnut-colored hair. His face, indeed, was like his body, flawless in proportions; and the unmanageable hair suggested the mane of a lion — a leonine head, a leonine nature formed to command. By his looks, by his voice, by his glance, he could have been picked among ten thousand chosen men.

It suddenly came to her that perhaps such a fellow, framed for superiority, might have chafed against the bonds of society, learned the fierce empire of the outlawed world, and have broken away to it.

"I thought," she said, deciding that frankness was entirely permissible with such a man, "that you would understand everything. I thought you wouldn't make friendly speeches that seem to require friendly answers. Because, you know, I have to do what I'm expected to do. If you want friendliness, I'll have to act the part. Is that the order?"

He smiled again, enjoying her mood.

"What's always queer to me about folks like you," he said, "clean-bred, clean-raised, clean-

128

taught, is that you ain't got the imagination to put yourselves in the boots of the other fellow. You see, we know we're a hard lot. We know you know it. But we figured you to have a sense of humor, lady. We figured you'd be able to forget what can't be helped for a day or two, and make yourself sociable. Understand?

"Back in the old days they had what they called The Truce of Heaven. I think it lasted from Thursday nights to Mondays. I dunno for sure, but a school-teacher told me about it once. Those were the times when every gent done his bit of fighting pretty regular and counted a week lost that didn't see him whaling away at some other gent in armor. Well, when Thursday night come, they quit the fighting. They laid off their armor and called on their enemies and sat down and had a smoke together, so to speak — because they wasn't any use talking mean and acting mean between Thursday and Monday. Well, I thought it was kind of the same way with us. Suppose it takes us a couple of days to dig that next hole. Does it pay for us to keep our claws out all the time during the two days? Can't we use the velvet paw, lady? Can't we call it The Truce of Heaven till we sink that hole and find out if the treasure of Cosslett is down under it."

"And if the treasure isn't there?"

"Then out come the claws. I have a bargain with your father, lady. You know that!"

She shuddered.

"But that's a good way off — two days, three

days — three centuries!" he suggested.

She nodded, intensely curious at this working of his mind.

"You'd gain one thing," he said. "If you'd give me your word not to try to leave and get to a town through the mountains, I'd parole you. Savvy?"

"You would accept my word?" she queried.

"As free as you'd accept mine," he answered at once.

She bit her lips to keep back the smile.

"I know," he said. "But when you come to think it over, you would take my word on anything. Go all through the mountains. That's what I'm known as — a gent that never busted a promise. Lot of other things charged up again' me, but never a real promise that I've broke."

"For instance," she said, "last night you promised that Ronicky Doone would be received as a friend, and yet your men opened fire on him!"

"Sure," he replied, absolutely unabashed. "I just stated that he'd be received that way. I didn't promise. I didn't take no oath. I didn't give anybody my hand on it."

She observed the distinction with a thoughtful mind. There was a distinction. Even the low took heed of the difference between an oath and a mere given word.

"It's hard for me to sympathize with that viewpoint," she said coldly. "In my world we could not call it fair play."

"I'm not asking for sympathy," he replied

readily. "Not a bit. I ain't asking you to step inside my world. But I want to find out if my world is so plumb far away from yours that you can't even see it through a telescope, so to speak. Is it?"

"No," she said, "I think I can understand a good many things. And I'll give you my word that I won't attempt to escape until —"

He did not wait for her to finish the difficult sentence.

"Mind shaking on that?" he said.

"No."

They shook hands. His palm was as soft as a woman's, well nigh. No labor had ever hardened it. For some reason the touch of that hand convinced her more than a thousand words, a thousand deeds, of the essential evil of the man.

"This is fine!" he said. "We'll have a couple of good days out of this. Why not? Every minute you save out of being sad, is a minute that's gained."

"But what if sorrow comes afterward?"

"Well, what happens to-morrow doesn't change what happens to-day."

It was the root, she felt, of his philosophy.

"I suppose not," she said cautiously. Then she became frank again. After all, he was distinctly worth frankness. Good or bad, he was a man. "Everything is very new to me here, as you understand. I'm trying to make it out."

"I wish you'd postpone judging me for a while," he begged. "Will you do that? I know it's hard for you to make me out. You can't know how a gent gets hungry to be free."

"I think I do know," she insisted. "I've met Ronicky Doone, and if ever there was a man who lives to be free, it is he!"

Her head went up with her enthusiasm; his head went down in thought, and he examined her with a keen glance.

"You figure he's a lot better than the ordinary, eh?"

"Don't you? But then, you don't know him."

"Lady," said the other, "I know him like a book."

"You've met him?"

"Never laid eyes on his face."

"You admit it!"

"I don't have to. I've heard about him. He's too important for me not to have heard. Gents like him and me can't live within a thousand miles of each other without knowing what the other fellow is."

"But he doesn't know you."

"Sure he don't. That's where he's weaker."

"Ah! Weaker?"

"That's what I said. He's got his parts. But he's too much of a fighter to be at the top of any game."

It was so absurd that she laughed. "You object to fighting?" she said.

"I wish you'd try to understand," he said, irritated. "You can if you want to. But you can't get all I mean with the first jump of your mind, every time. Sure I object to fighting.

That's a last resource. Gents that do nothing but fight their way into trouble and out of it, are like wolves. No better. They're beasts. Maybe fine beasts, but beasts just the same. What makes men different? Brains, lady, brains! It ain't how hard a gent can hit or how quick and straight he can shoot. It's what he's got above the eyes. Understand me?"

"Of course I understand you; and of course I agree." She was piqued by his bluntness. And yet at the same time it made her wish more than ever to have his respect. The respect of Jack Moon! Afterward, she would marvel at herself and her mood during that talk! "But you have to admit that it sounds queer coming from Jack Moon."

"Sure — Jack Moon the way you know him now. Not the Jack Moon I hope you'll get to know."

"Do you really want me to know you? Wouldn't you be less strong, less invincible, if any one really understood you?"

"You won't," said he calmly. "But I'm going to show you my insides if I can. The more you show of yourself the more people miss you."

"Where are your weaknesses?" she said.

"That's asking. But I'll tell you. I'm vain. I like to be flattered."

"But you intend to be forearmed, I see!"

"Don't do any good to be prepared for a thing. That's my weakness. You'd laugh if you knew the way it works. Ain't a man in my crowd that I don't want to have respect me. If I can't get 'em to love me, I want 'em to fear me; and you can lay to it that they all do!"

"And that flatters you?"

"Of course. Take you, for instance. If I can't make you like me — like to talk to me; of course I don't mean anything more'n that — then the next best is to have you shake every time I come near you."

She looked at him out of narrowed eyes. And she knew that the fellow was actually telling the truth! And yet the door he had opened let in only enough light upon his involute nature to give her a deceptive feeling of knowledge. The main theme — the key to the mystery — was still farther beyond.

"A little knowledge is a dangerous thing, I'm afraid," she said. "I'm not going to use what I know."

"Thanks," said the outlaw. "Here we are almost home!"

The clearing of the shacks was before them, and the crowd, which had hurried on ahead of them, was already busy at twenty preparations for the night and the evening meal. The sunset was touching only the tops of the trees now. All beneath was swiftly deepening shadow.

"However," she said as a parting shot, "I'm going to maintain that there are two types of freedom — yours and Ronicky's!"

"You know him well enough to call him Ronicky?"

"Yes."

134

"And he calls you Jerry!"

"Why not?"

"No harm. Well, I tell you what: I could take this Ronicky Doone and wind him around my finger. I could make him my man! I could get him into my crowd if I wanted to!"

She flushed with her anger.

"That's simply impossible! Ronicky Doone? He's the soul of everything honorable!"

"Actions speak, lady," and Jack Moon grinned. "Suppose I was to go out and bring him into this camp!"

"You could only bring him dead!"

"That so? I'd bet on it, though."

"As a member of your band?"

"That's what I said. Have him in here sleeping right along with the rest of the boys. He'd take Harry Bush's place!"

"You can't do it, Jack Moon! I — unless you're a hypnotist."

"You're weakening," said the other coldly. "Must be kind of fond of this gent if you can't believe anything wrong about him!"

"I'll tell you this," she said firmly. "If he came down here as a member of your band, I'd despise him with all my heart. I'd loathe him!"

"That's hard on me," remarked Jack Moon. "But it sounds to me like a bet. What say? Shall I go out and try to get him down here?"

"If you go to face him, you'd risk your life!"

"Not the first time. Besides, it'd be worth it."

"How?"

135

"To see your face when I bring him in. Shall I try?"

"You'll gain nothing from me, sir!" She was trembling with excitement. "But go out. Try him. If he's as weak as that, then there's no steady faith, no honesty, no truth in any man in the world! But how — how could you get him?"

"Ain't there gold over yonder? Wouldn't he like a share in it?"

"You'd buy him!"

"They say everybody has a price, and I can bid pretty high right now!"

"You'll fail, Jack Moon!"

He laughed mockingly and turned abruptly on his heel and strode out into the shade of the trees.

# CHAPTER XVI

## BROKEN FAITH

His first hundred yards were made at a rapid pace, but after that, finding himself entirely alone and well out of possible observation from behind, he reduced his gait and went on more slowly, more cautiously, keeping a sharp lookout through the tree trunks around him. Indeed, so sensitive had he suddenly become that now and again he paused and whirled toward the movement of a wind-swayed sapling or the swing of a bough. His progress, however, was fairly steady. He paused only to break off a slender dead branch some six feet long, and at the top of this he tied a white handkerchief.

In this wise he broke from the trees and came into the clearing at the bottom of the hollow. He must now be well beyond earshot of the camp, and suddenly he began to shout: "Doone! Ronicky Doone! Oh, Doone!"

He repeated the call in a high and piercing wail several times, and yet it was strange that he should expect the man to come to what might well be considered a trap. Strange, too, that he should expect to find him so near the scene of danger. Yet at the third repetition of the call a voice spoke behind him.

"I'm here. What's the racket about?"

He turned slowly, very slowly. It was a maxim with him that quick moves are very dangerous.

He found himself looking at Ronicky Doone, though the latter was so covered with a mottling of shadows that he was almost rendered invisible. It was a sort of protective coloration — or shadowing, to be more accurate.

"Been following me long?" said the outlaw, leaning on his branch.

"Only since you started away from the shacks," said Ronicky.

"Well, well," and Moon sighed, "you sure are handy in a forest. Must of learned young."

"Tolerable."

"Ain't it kind of dangerous trusting yourself on foot, when we got so many men to cut in around you on hossback?"

As a reply Ronicky whistled very softly, so softly that it barely reached the ears of the bandit leader, and out of the denser night of the trees behind Ronicky came the form of Lou. She was almost lost in the sea of shadow. Only her head, with the pricking ears and the bright eyes, appeared at the shoulder of her master.

"By Jiminy!" exclaimed Jack Moon, smiling with an almost boyish pleasure. "That's sure a hoss, that one of yours. Lou?"

"You've heard of her?"

"Everybody that's heard of you has heard of

her, if they have any ears to listen to folks' talk," said the other. "She's handy herself, ain't she? How come she don't make any more noise going through a wood?"

"Training," answered Ronicky Doone. "Took a pile of pains."

"I reckon!"

"But now she knows enough not to step where the dead leaves are thick or on a branch or nothing like that. Besides, I've got her so's she knows when she ain't to make any noise like whinnying."

"That must of took time, Ronicky!"

"About two years, training her every day."

"You don't say! Well, you sure are the out-beatingest gent for patience, Ronicky!"

The other returned no answer. It was very strange to hear them conversing in so frank a manner, making no mysteries with each other — the one asking simple questions, the other answering them with fully as much simplicity. One might have thought them old and familiar acquaintances. Neither had raised his voice since Ronicky answered the third call.

"How come you to foller so close?" went on Jack Moon.

"I'm going to kill you, Moon," said the smaller man, as gentle of voice as ever.

"The devil you are!" murmured Moon, also without violence. "How come?"

"They won't hear the gun. Not with that wood-chopping going on and at this distance."

"No, maybe not. And then what?"

"Hide your body and then drift back to the camp and get Dawn and the girl to-night."

"You agin' a dozen?"

"A dozen? They's only a man and a half in that camp. And you're the whole man, partner."

"I take that kind of you, Ronicky."

"Don't mention it."

"But they'll have numbers on you!"

"Numbers ain't anything. Not in night work. Not when you got the instinct for shooting. I'd sort of like it."

"You would?"

"Yep. I never met up with so many gents that was all ripe for shooting, Moon. And I sure would like to get busy right among all them targets."

"Why don't you get a job with a sheriff?" asked Moon. "That'd keep your hand in on the work you like."

"I wouldn't make it professional. I ain't that low. I shoot to kill when I have to, that's all."

"But you sort of like to have to, eh?"

"I guess that's it. Ah!"

The last monosyllable was a snarl of eagerness, and the hand of Ronicky flashed down to his revolver — but it came away again and rested carelessly on his hip. He had mistaken a movement of the outlaw's right hand.

"Sorry," said Ronicky.

"That's all right. I got steady nerves. Well, Ronicky, it's sure fine to have met you after hearing so much about you. And it's fine to see you so fit."

"Thanks," said Ronicky. "I'm waiting for you to start something, Jack."

"Want me to start for my gat first? I never take gifts, Ronicky. They cost too much!"

"H'm!" said Ronicky. "You're a queer bird, Jack."

"Yep. That's right. I'm queer. Pretty near as queer as you. You're so sure you'd beat me if we come to pulling guns."

"That ain't queer," said Ronicky. "It's just a feeling you get."

"Like shooting in the dark?"

"Kind of. I know I'm a faster man than you, Jack. Shooting you is pretty near to murder — except that you been such a devil that you deserve a thousand killings."

"Thanks! But they ain't going to be no gun play, son."

"No?"

"I've said they wasn't, and I mean it. You're going to come back in camp with me. You're going to come back as one of my men."

Ronicky started and then shook his head.

"You got me figured all wrong," he said patiently. "I ain't your kind, Jack."

"Nobody is," said the other. "But you'll come."

"To get a share of the Cosslett gold if it's found?"

"D'you think I'd try to buy you with gold, Ronicky? Son, you must think I'm a plumb fool. No, money ain't your price."

"I got a price, have I?"

"I'll show you. You'll come into camp with me because you want to get Dawn and the girl off."

"Well? Ain't they made a bargain? They show you the treasure, and you set 'em free."

"You know as well as me that they ain't any treasure, son. I'm digging just for the fun of it. One chance in a thousand, maybe, and it's worth the try."

"Moon," said the other, straightening, "it ain't any good. I know you."

"You're the only gent in the world that does, then," said Jack Moon.

"Maybe you think that. Maybe you're right. I don't want to get close enough to a gent like you to find out the truth. I want to put on gloves when I handle you."

"That's sort of strong, son!"

"Curse you!" said Ronicky Doone, his voice trembling suddenly with a horror and loathing which he had been repressing all of this time, "I can understand and forgive some gents for killing. Some men kill because they go plumb mad with anger. And I'd forgive them. But you — you're never going to lose your temper. You're not fond of nothing but yourself. You kill because things get in your way. You kill by rule, the way other folks build a house or do 'rithmetic. Moon, of all the gents I ever hear about, you're the worst. I'm going to finish you, right here under these trees!"

"Sure sorry!" the outlaw chuckled. "But, Ronicky, I won't fight!"

The other gasped.

"You? Not fight? Jack Moon not fight?"

"That's what I said."

"You lie!"

"Nope. Why should I get myself dropped? Right now I know you're a better man than I am."

"Moon, I'm going to pull my gun. Defend yourself like a man, or I'll shoot you like the skunk you are!"

But Jack Moon dropped both hands on his hips and smiled straight at the set face of Ronicky Doone.

"You can't do it, Ronicky," he said. "That's the trouble with fools like you. You can't do a lot of things you ought to do. You won't shoot till I move for my gun. I ain't going to move!"

"I'll let the mountains know you're yaller, Moon!"

"Tell the mountains, then. None of the men would believe it."

Ronicky Doone ground his teeth, knowing the truth.

"Come out with your game, Jack," he said at last. "How you going to get me? Why d'you want me? How come you think I'm such a fool I'll go into your camp with you where I'd be helpless?"

The leader laughed softly, more to himself — an inward mirth.

"D'you expect me to answer all them questions? All I'll tell you is this: I'm going to get you into camp so's I can down you by myself, Ronicky. You're a better man than me right now. The first

I've ever met! But after I've had you with me for twenty-four hours, you'll begin to get weak — without knowing it. And when the bust comes, I'll win! That's the main reason!"

"You think I'm a plumb fool, Jack," said Ronicky. "Come into your camp? What'd make me want to do that?"

"Because you're weak in the head," said the outlaw, with the utmost calm. "You took up Dawn's fight for no good reason, and now you got to fight it through, or you can't never respect yourself again. And the only way you can help Dawn is by getting into camp, where you and Dawn can try to make your break side by side or fight us to the finish back to back! You know that, and that's why you'll take my offer. You talk about rushing the camp at night. That's fool talk. You know's well as I know that the first shot fired would be by my man Treat into the head of Hugh Dawn."

Ronicky glowered. Indeed, the bait was almost irresistible, even though he was warned at the same time that, if he took it, the trap would close over him sooner or later.

"You can come in with me," said Jack Moon, "but when you come, you got to act like one of my men. And I'll make them like it! They'll want to finish you the first week or so. But you'll take care of that. I trust you to sort of make your own way!"

He grinned at Ronicky with malevolent meaning.

144

"Suppose I was to start a riot and shoot up some of your men, Jack? Think about that?"

"You won't do it. You ain't the kind that can kill without cause. You'll just bluff them down."

Suddenly Ronicky started.

"Suppose I was to take up your offer — which I ain't going to do, of course — what would Dawn and the girl think, not knowing the truth, and thinking that I've took the oath and become one of your men? I didn't think of that before!"

"They'll think you're a skunk," said Jack Moon. "That's the main reason I want to get you there. The girl's too fond of you."

Again Ronicky started.

"Talk soft about her," he said fiercely.

"Sure," and the outlaw nodded. "I like her fine. No fear of me talking hard about her. Matter of fact, I'm bringing you in so's I can show her that I've done what I told her I'd do — wind you right around my little finger!"

"You swine!" muttered Ronicky.

"What difference does that make? Even if she despises you for a couple of days, won't you still have your chance to play hero later on and save her and her father? And when you get away with them, can't you explain how everything lies?" He paused, then added: "But while you're in camp you'll explain nothing to nobody. I'll have your word on that before you go in!"

"I'm not going in," said Ronicky. "I got a little sense left!"

"You're afraid I'll hypnotize you, or something?" said the leader. "Afraid of my men? Far as that goes, I'll give you my word that I won't let the crowd jump you. A couple might try to measure you, but you can take care of yourself, I reckon. Later on, when I'm ready, you and me'll have it out! Make your play, Ronicky. Will you come, or will you just hang around here in the trees and do no good? You can't get help. You know I got enough on Dawn to have him sent up or executed along with me if we're caught. And I'd sure bust myself wide open to do it. One down, all down. That's my motto."

Ronicky sighed. "I'm coming," he said. "I'm coming, Jack. I start in feeling that I'm beat. You're too clever for me. But I ain't going to admit I'm beat till you drop me full of lead as a roast is full of cloves. Lead on, partner."

"You understand everything?"

"I go in and let on that I've took the oath to stick with your crowd."

"And you promise that you won't use what you might learn from the boys if they should get to talking promiscuous to you about what we've done in the old days."

"I'll promise that. I'm not to do any explaining to anybody, the girl in particular. I'm to work under your orders until I get my chance to make my own play. Same time you contract that you won't send your whole crowd after me. That's what we shake on?"

"That's what we shake on. The only showdown will be between you and me. The girl —"

"Leave her out," said Ronicky sharply.

The other laughed. "Anyway you want. But I'm going to show her that I'm a better man than you are."

"She's got too much sense not to see through you, Moon!"

"Has she? I like 'em clever, Doone. They play better into my hand when they're that way! Do we shake hands and start back?"

Ronicky bowed his head, though never for an instant taking his eyes off the big figure in front of him. A few minutes before he had been on the point of drawing his revolver and shooting to kill. But the man had bound his arms with an invisible cord and had netted him in an hypnotic influence. He felt that to bow to the will of the outlaw would be disastrous. Yet, was it not cowardice to refuse? Was there really anything to dread save mob action on the part of the crowd? If he could trust Moon's word to prevent such action, what else was there to worry over? In the meantime, the man to whom he had given his promise that he would see him through to the end, was a helpless, hopeless prisoner in the midst of the band.

"I'll go," said Ronicky at last, "on your own terms. You take me in to prove to the girl that I'm crooked. I accept because I want to get the girl and her father loose. We both have our eyes open — we play the game — we hope to plant each other under the sod in the end. Let's start back!"

"Good!" said the outlaw, and, stepping briskly

147

forth to lead the way, he began laughing softly to himself.

As for Ronicky, his mind was in a whirl of doubts as he followed. This was not his sphere, this atmosphere of trickery and suspicion. He was meant for swift decisions swiftly acted upon. But, having committed himself to this course of action, he could do nothing but submit and let chance bring what it would. At least, he could be constantly on the alert, and if Moon strove to strike by surprise the blow might recoil on his own head.

They came to the edge of the clearing. The shacks were indistinct masses of shadow now, save for the faces on which the firelight struck. A mass of dead logs had been heaped in the center of the open space, and the flames from them leaped straight up until the wind, which stirred above the treetops, lopped off the fire in great billows and extinguished them in waves of darkness.

This fire was for the purpose of giving heat, as the night was coming on chill; the cooking fire was a much humbler affair drawn well to one side. Scattered about it was the expectant circle. What Ronicky Doone saw was a blur of strong, ill-shaven faces, alternately played upon by light and shade as the men leaned toward the fire or sat back. Next he saw the shining hair of the girl, turning to red gold where the firelight struck through it.

She sat with her fingers locked about her knees, and she was talking with animation to the solemn-faced Silas Treat, her nearest neighbor on the right. Hugh Dawn flanked her on the other side.

"Looks kind of at home already, don't she?" asked Jack Moon. "She's one in a thousand, that girl!"

"Sure," said Ronicky Doone. "She's smart enough to know how to act a part."

But he was ill at ease. If in five minutes the outlaw leader had been able to change the mind of a man bent on killing him, and had brought the would-be combatant peaceably back to his camp and really into his power, what could he not do with a girl of an impressionable age? Something must be done about this. The girl must be warned sharply to be on her guard, not against physical danger, because that could not exist among Westerners for her, but against the insidious words of Jack Moon.

It seemed that Moon read his thoughts and defied him.

"I'll make a place for you between Treat and the girl," he said. "You see, I figure to keep you happy, Ronicky!"

He stepped forward to the girl, and Ronicky saw her lift her head with a start and then stare beyond the leader into the darkness. Seeing no one — perhaps the firelight blinded her — she laughed and seemed highly pleased. Then he made out Moon's voice saying: "Thought you'd be getting lonely, maybe, among all us rough gents. So I brought you a friend."

At that she started to her feet, and Ronicky came on toward her, smiling. At sight of him she stiffened, at first as though in horror, and then with an exclamation of scorn which Ronicky Doone was never to forget.

"Don't come near me!" she cried fiercely. "Don't come near me! Jack Moon, I'd rather have any member of your crew beside me than that — creature! I thought there was one man in the world who valued himself above a price. But now I see there's none. None!"

"Jerry," said Ronicky eagerly, "inside of three days you'll know the truth about this."

"For money!" breathed the girl, white of face. "Sold for money! Why, a man like Jack Moon who defies the law is far finer than you! At least he isn't sold. He may buy, but he's never bought!"

"I could talk forever now," said Ronicky, "and never show you why I'm here. But when the time comes, you'll know."

"Whatever you say," she replied, "remember this: I don't care to hear you. You've sold more than yourself. You've sold my faith in you. And that can be sold only once. This is the last word I'll address to you, sir!"

She turned her back and sat down.

"I didn't figure," said Jack Moon, "that you'd come so close to saying kind things about me so soon."

"Kind?" she answered. Suddenly her anger melted almost to the point of tears. "Don't you see I hate you for what you've done to him? It — it's worse than killing a man. It's devilish, this buying of a soul!"

# CHAPTER XVII

## REWARD OF SERVICE

But the leader seemed quite unperturbed by her words. He turned cheerfully to the circle of men, and they interrupted their own talk to stare at the newcomer.

"Gents," said Moon, "this is Ronicky Doone. I've brought him around to our way of thinking. I want you to take to him, and I'm pretty sure that he'll take to us. I guess they ain't anybody here that'd vote agin' letting Ronicky have a share of the plunder if we find Cosslett's gold. If they is, speak up!"

Ronicky could see the point of this speech. Without making a definite statement, the bandit allowed it to be clearly inferred that the offer of a share in the gold had been the purchase price of the new member of the band. Now the wave of silence traveled around the circle, and keen eyes looked at him from under grimly gathered brows.

Silas Treat spoke first. "This kid looks tolerable young to me. I got a right to talk. Any gent that's brought in may be sent out with me to do a little job later on. I want to know what he'll turn when it comes to taking a trick. How does he ride? How does he shoot? What does he know? What's he done?"

"I'll answer that," said the leader. "First place, I'll answer for him as a fighting man. They ain't such a thing as luck in a gun play. Or if there is, lucky gents are what we want. I've heard about Doone for two years. Take too long to tell you all. But the first of you that gets tangled with him, will find out a bunch of things pronto. About the rest — well, call your hoss, Ronicky!"

Wondering what point there could be in this, Ronicky whistled sharply, and from behind came the swift beating of hoofs. The bay mare shot into the circle of the firelight and stood, a gleaming, beautiful figure, beside her master. There she fidgeted, turning this way and that and eying the bandits with uneasy glances, as though she were not at all pleased to find her owner in such company.

"Look her over, boys," said Moon. "Is they a hoss in the outfit that can touch her? Is a hoss like that ever going to be run down on the trail? And can't you judge a gent pretty much by the hoss he rides?"

These words were to a large degree drowned by the murmur which had risen simultaneously from many throats, drawn forth by the exquisite lines of Lou. All doubt at once vanished.

"Glad to see you, pal," said Silas Treat, advancing across the circle until he loomed huge above Ronicky, and he stretched forth his hand. It was not taken, and Treat drew himself back a pace.

"Gents," said Ronicky, "I sure appreciate being

152

taken in. But you don't know me yet. Wait till you've found out what I am. If you feel the same way then — why, we'll shake hands. But you can't tell in the beginning of some things how they're going to end. Just leave this up in the air. Later on — well, we'll know each other a pile better!"

The speech was well received, particularly by Silas Treat.

"That sounds like more sense than I figure on hearing out of a gent ten years older than you, son," he declared. "All right. We'll try you out, but I aim to say that I think you'll live up to standard fine! How about it, boys?"

There was a growl of assent. The bright eyes still probed suspiciously at Ronicky, but there was a willingness now to find some measure of good in him. But Ronicky was delighted because he had avoided giving his hand to the whole circle. That would have tied him down. Now he was frankly on trial with the band and the band was on trial with him. He glanced at Moon and saw that the leader was biting his lips in vexation. He, at least, was clever enough to understand the meaning of Ronicky's maneuver.

In the meantime, Ronicky sat down, withdrawing a little from the intimate, inner circle about the fire. He looked squarely across at the girl. She was talking quite gayly with her father. Now and then some one of the men addressed a remark to her, and she answered. But always, in flitting here and there, her glance became a blank when it passed over the spot where Ronicky was sitting.

This hurt him; and the injustice was inclined to make him sulk. Yet he could not help admiring her, even impersonally. Here, playing her part among men who might, within two or three days, be the murderers of her father, striving with all her force to gain such a hold upon them that in the crisis she might be able to turn them from their purpose, she was at her very best. Firelight had turned the sand-colored hair to a rich gold; excitement brought color to her cheeks and set her eyes gleaming.

"Look here," said a voice from the far side of the circle. "Ain't you going to change seats after a while, Treat? D'you sit beside the lady all evening?"

"I ain't heard her shouting out loud for you to come and rescue her," said Treat.

"You see," explained the girl, "I plan to take Si back with me."

"And why not me, too?" came a chorus.

"Because you're all known men," she answered. "But Si carries his mask about with him."

Silas Treat stroked the dense mustaches and beard which had inspired the remark and grinned down at the girl. As the laughter died, Baldy McNair slipped into a place beside Ronicky.

"You were lying up in the barn the other night," he said. "You heard me and Marty talking, I understand?"

"That's it."

"And that was what started you going?"

"Yep."

Baldy McNair sighed.

"Well," he murmured at length, "you started on the trail of doing a pretty good thing. I'm sort of sorry, partner, to see you wind up in this joint. But — that ain't my business."

Ronicky looked steadily into the open eyes of the ruddy-faced man.

"I'll get to know you better," he said. "I'd like to, a pile."

In the meantime, the outlaw chief had taken a place just behind Jerry Dawn, and gradually he drew her attention away from the circle and into earnest conversation with himself. Ronicky noted the changes from positive distaste, which she could barely conquer at first, to interest and then even to excitement. What they said was pitched well beneath the sustained chatter of the men, but by the expression of the girl Ronicky knew that she was by no means unhappy in the company of Moon.

He shook his head in wonder. It seemed utterly impossible that she could stay near him for an instant — near this man whose known crimes were too numerous for memory, and whose unknown deeds made probably an even blacker record. But he knew that women have strange powers of forgetfulness. The past of Jack Moon no doubt was beginning to grow dim in her mind. The present was all she was capable of knowing. Even the future danger impending over her father was probably forgotten for the moment. All she saw, all she heard, were the handsome face, the smooth voice of Jack Moon, leader of men.

Indeed, between a king and the ruler of a pirate crew there is a similarity. To be a single robber is a despicable thing; to be a mighty leader of robbers is to be — a Tamerlane, perhaps. And if Jack Moon were not in the latter class, he was certainly not in the first. An air of superiority clothed him. Among such fellows as these, he seemed a giant. When the thought of his crimes obtruded, might she not be tempted to a greater pity than condemnation? Hitherto he had struck no one of hers. Her father was still safe. And as to what he had done in the rest of the world, were not all women full of forgiveness for handsome, smooth-tongued rascals?

Sick at heart, finally he turned away and stepped out into the darkness of the trees. This, then, was the reward of service!

Ronicky could gladly have walked on through the forest and the night, and left it all behind him. What had happened to Jerry Dawn? What had come of her trust in him, her enthusiastic admiration? Now she seemed to regard the outlaw chief, terrible Jack Moon, as a friend!

If that were her attitude, was it not better to shake the whole matter from his attention and let Hugh Dawn and his daughter solve their own problem? One thing held him, and that a potent chain — his word passed to Dawn to see him through the trouble.

Accordingly he came back and entered the clearing. Things were rapidly settling down for the night, since most of the men were worn out by the labors of the day. Half a dozen were already preparing their bunks in the shacks. Moon stood in front of the little hut which had been reserved for Jerry Dawn, and he was talking with the girl before she went in to sleep. Her father sat entirely alone — but watched by how many wolfish eyes! — near the fire.

Ronicky went straight to him and sat down at his side.

"Hugh," he said, "what's come over Jerry? Has she lost her head? Has she gone mad, talking to Moon like that? Look at 'em over there! You'd think he wasn't himself. You'd think he wasn't planning to get your scalp if he can! You'd think he was an old family friend or a suitor, or something like that!"

Hugh Dawn did not turn his head. But he smiled sorrowfully at the younger man.

"It's Moon getting in his work," he said. "You can't beat Jack Moon! No way of doing it!"

"That's foolish talk! Anybody can be beaten!"

"Can they? Well, maybe. I don't pretend to know everything."

"Moon has the strength of twelve men behind him. Thirteen to two is the odds against us. Little more than six to one is hard odds, but it's been beat before."

"He's got more than that on his side, son. He's

got our weaknesses."

Ronicky Doone, after all, was very young, very impetuous, and not extremely thoughtful. "I don't follow that," he admitted.

"I'll show you," said Hugh. "What's your weakness and Jerry's weakness, far as Jack's concerned? Your honor. Your word's good, and so's hers. He's made you promise something — I don't know what. Anyway, he's brought you in here, and he's keeping you. And he's got Jerry to promise not to try to run away."

"But what could he do if she did run away? What could I do? How can we bring help? The minute outsiders come, Moon would put a bullet through your head. She knows it; I know it."

"Sure. Maybe that's what Moon's worked on. Anyway, he's done it. He's tying your hands with your weaknesses."

"But Moon's own word is good as gold. You told me so yourself."

"Sure it is. Because his price has never been bid."

"But doesn't Jerry realize what you understand — that though I seem to be down here as one of Moon's men —"

He stopped, realizing that his promise to Moon kept him from explaining.

"She ain't the reasoning kind," said the older man. "She jumps to a conclusion the way a hoss jumps a fence into a new pasture. All she knows is that you're here, and that you seem to be one of Moon's men."

158

"But she talks to Moon like a friend, yet she sure knows that he's a murderer a hundred times over!"

"She's never seen him do a murder. And the things that count with women are the things they've seen. They're a practical lot, and you can lay to that. She thought Moon was a skunk at first. That was because she liked you. Now she thinks you're one of Moon's men, and so you're worse than Moon. How Jack got you, I don't ask. You're here and that's the main point."

"But, man, will you put in a word with her for me?"

"It's no good. Moon's got her all trained against you." It was strange to see the big fellow surrender so entirely to the very presence of the outlaw chief. All hope seemed to have left.

"It'll come out right in the end," insisted Ronicky. "You have his word that if the gold's found, you go free."

"His word? He'll find a way to keep me. Think he'll give me up, knowing that when I leave Jerry goes with me and he sees the last of her?"

Ronicky gasped.

"You think he wants to — to marry her?"

"I dunno. I've never known him to waste time on a girl before. Jerry's the first."

Sweat stood out on the forehead of Ronicky. At last he muttered: "Anyway, you're safe as long's she's with you here!"

"Safe?" Hugh Dawn laughed without mirth. "You wait and see. A gun'll go off by accident, in the end — or a rock'll roll down a hill as I'm walking beneath it. That's the way it'll happen."

"Then," cried Ronicky, "let's you and me pull out guns and grab the girl and make a break for it! Are you going to stay and get murdered?"

"No use," and Hugh Dawn sighed. "I'm watched. I couldn't run a step without getting dropped. Same way with you. You can't beat Jack Moon!"

# CHAPTER XVIII

# GOLD!

The little camp awakened to a swirl of activity in the morning. Whatever were the problems of Dawn and Ronicky, the rest of the crowd was interested in gold. Gold had haunted their dreams. Gold wakened them in the first gray of dawn. Gold drove them through a hasty breakfast, and for the sake of gold their picks and shovels were deep in the dirt in the hollow well before sunrise.

Their united efforts had rolled away the boulders which were scattered over the surface of the designated spot. Below, they found a soft soil, and the hole sank rapidly. Five feet down, however, they struck a dense layer of clay, which had to be chewed out bit by bit with picks.

The laborers paused, growling, but Jack Moon himself leaped down into the pit and caught up a pick. The others now fell to with a will, and an hour of terrific labor pierced the clay and let them down again into gravel and sand.

They had driven through the depth of the mound which the landslide had tumbled over the place, when the sun rose red through the eastern trees, and now, warming to the work, they pushed

161

the hole deeper and deeper.

Learning from the experience of the first pit, they made the excavation this second time much wider at the top and sank it in two steps, from each of which, when the bottom was reached, they could pass the soil in relays to the surface. By noon they were down a full fifteen feet below the true surface of the ground, and now the entire crowd was at work at the same time. The pace was slower than when they worked in shifts, but the progress downward was more steady, a continuous stream of sand and gravel pouring over the lip of the pit as it was deepened below.

Two men brought down provisions for a quick lunch, and in ten minutes the work was resumed. For there was great need of haste. Never before had the band of Jack Moon been retained so long in one place. The long immunity which Moon and his followers had enjoyed was indubitably owing to the swiftness with which they gathered, worked, and dispersed, each man to a separate quarter. One day together was comparatively safe. Two became rash. And to spend three days together was actually putting one's head in the noose. This being the third day of their assemblage, and the second they had camped on one spot, there was not only love of gold but fear of death to spur them on.

Mid-afternoon saw them down to twenty feet; but now they were working through a dense stratum, and the progress was slow. Besides, the whole crowd, from Hugh Dawn to Ronicky, was exhausted.

Suddenly there was a yell from little Bud Kent as he jerked something from the ground with his shovel. He had pried up an ancient pick, and now he raised it above his head, the iron a mass of black rust, and the haft sadly decayed. But it was proof positive that they were not on a blind trail. Some one had dug here before!

Who thought of weariness now? On they went with a shout and a roar. The gravel and sand flew up in a ceaseless shower. A dozen backs were rising and falling swiftly. The pebbles chimed and rang as they whipped up from the polished shovel blades.

It was exactly half past four when the next sensation came. They were down a shade more than twenty-two feet when Jack Moon, again in the pit, raised, without a word, poising it high on his shovel — the blackened skull of a man.

That hideous specter cast a blanket of silence over the group, then a groan of disappointment. Jerry had turned away, sick.

"Nothing more!" Bud Kent remarked in disgust. "Maybe old Cosslett did dig this hole and dug it deep; but it was only because he wanted to get this gent out of sight. It's a burial ground, not a treasure cache. Boys, we're through!"

"Wait a minute, Bud," called Jack Moon. "Look here. There's a nice little hole drilled through this skull between the eyes. Took a bullet to do that, son. What did somebody say awhile back? That Cosslett might of had a couple of gents dig this

163

hole and then shot them into it and covered the bodies up? Well?"

That possible explanation at least gave them renewed hope. Labor began again. And in ten minutes they had uncovered and removed two complete skeletons!

Still the hole sank to twenty-three feet, twenty-three and a half, twenty-four, twenty-four and a half! Not a word had been spoken, now, for an hour. Lanterns had been brought and were lighted, ready for use as the evening came on. And already their glow began to be as bright as the twilight.

Presently from Corrigan, a big brute of a man, wielding a shovel with steady might, came a dull roar of excitement. The gravel flew up from his blade as the others in the narrow pit stood back. Then, from the three workers in those cramped quarters, came a single-throated wail of excitement. The scraping shovel had cleaned off the top of an iron-bound chest!

The yelling from the bottom of the hole was redoubled by the echoes along the sides of the pit and raised again by the men working at the mouth. They crowded about it as Jack Moon, with a hoarse shout, called to those below to make way for him.

Next instant he was down into the bottom of the pit, and wrenched a pick from the hands of one of the diggers, and, sinking it through the top boards of the chest, had torn one of them up. Below was a quantity of cloth or canvas. One slash of his knife divided it. Then by the light of the lanterns which had been lowered from the surface as far as possible, every eye at once caught the gleam and glitter of yellow — the unmistakable shimmer of gold!

The heart of the girl swelled until she could hardly breathe as she waited for the shouts of rejoicing. But not one came. Men were trembling, wild of eye, but their loudest voice was a husky whisper. Only Jack Moon was speaking aloud, and he was ordering them to pass the stuff up to the surface. It rose from shaking hand to shaking hand, and up on the lip of the pit came a gathering heap of gold spilling at the feet of the girl. She gazed on it, incredulous.

There was power, happiness, freedom in that growing heap of yellow. It was an arm to pursue and a strong hand to support. It could reward and punish. It could actually buy a life. How many, indeed, had already been paid down freely to win this same metal from the earth, to take it again from the rightful owners, and, last of all, to hide it?

Her father, frantic with joy, clambered from the pit, kneeled by the mass, buried his hands in it, and then looked up to her with a maniacal laugh! Others were coming up. The chest had been gutted of its contents. And as fast as they reached the top of the ground, hand after hand, shaking with joy, was buried in the treasure. Then Baldy McNair broke the charm.

"Get down again, boys!" he cried. "This is only the beginning. There's a ton of gold here. But what's that? Not seven hundred thousand dollars!

There must be more — ten times as much — maybe twenty times as much! Who knows? Come down again and dig!"

But the heavy voice of the leader answered him as Jack Moon climbed up from the pit.

"Hold the lanterns out. Look down yonder," he commanded.

They obeyed. The chest had been smashed to pieces by Moon and put to one side, and in the clear place below it they saw the wet glimmer of bed rock.

"There's no more," explained Moon. "One dollar of gold always makes ten dollars' worth of talk. And there you are! You'll find no more treasure. That's what Cosslett put down under ground, and that's all he got. The rest is just talk — that I believed like a fool. But ain't this enough? Over six hundred thousand dollars, boys. Split that by twenty, for example — there you have thirty-three thousand dollars apiece. Is it enough?"

They had been promised ten times that much before. But half a million in talk did not equal the actuality of less than a tenth of that in sheer gold. On the damp pile of sand on the edge of the pit they apportioned the loot, with the aid of a pocket scales. There was a share for each of Moon's twelve men, and for the leader himself three shares. To Ronicky and Dawn went also a share apiece. Seventeen shares, then, were apportioned.

Full darkness came while Moon still weighed and apportioned the gold with his scales. The dust had been hammered into small bars of every conceivable shape for the sake of security in handling, and now the men put their shares away in saddlebags or pieces of the canvas which had been used to cover the treasure in the chest, and some even divided the loot in small pieces and put it in their pockets.

And so at length they started up the hill for their camp, staggering under their burdens, yelling and singing as they walked, for all the world like a procession of wild drunkards. Corrigan helped the leader bear the crushing burden of his own portion.

On the way Moon found an opportunity to drop back to the side of Jerry Dawn.

"Don't worry," he said softly. "I'll find a means of getting all this into the hands of the gent to whom it belongs — your father!"

"No, no!" whispered the girl, by this time completely misled. "You mustn't dream of it! They'd do murder before they'd give it up. Besides, we're amply repaid!"

"Tush!" Jack Moon smiled. "There's ways of handling these gents. And I know all the ways!"

# CHAPTER XIX

## DOONE'S SHARE

Hunger, thirst, and food were forgotten in the excitement that followed the division of the gold. Only the cursing and the fierce commands of Jack Moon made his followers build a big fire and prepare a hasty supper. It was eaten by some, uneaten by others. The shouting and singing had no end. And the quick, bright, covetous glances were continually traveling toward the stores of neighbors.

Ronicky Doone found Hugh and his daughter a little removed. He dropped his canvas bag with its precious contents of gold at the feet of Dawn.

"I never would of taken it in the first place," he said simply, "except to get more for you. There you are and welcome, Hugh; and if I could get more away from 'em and give it to you, I would. It's yours by right."

Hugh Dawn clutched the bag, his eyes glittering.

"Son," he said, "I've always swore by you. But this is just too much, and —"

His daughter drew his hands from the canvas.

"Dad!" she cried in shame. "You're not going to take it?"

"It's his," said Ronicky cheerfully. "It's his — or else it lies there where it is. I don't want it!"

"You don't want it?" echoed the girl, staring up to him.

Money had always been scant and hard earned in her life. She saw this fellow giving her father what was the equivalent of the salary of forty years of school teaching, and her head turned at the mere thought of it.

"I don't want it," said Ronicky firmly. "Tell you why. I don't figure a gent can ever get something for nothing. If you're going to get money, you got to work for it some way. What work have I done to get this? Nope, I don't want it."

"You've worked as much as any one," said Hugh Dawn, urged on by a glance of his daughter to refuse the money.

"Well," said Ronicky, "even if I have, I don't want it. They's been too many lives lost over the stuff to suit me. You take my share, partner. You couldn't force the stuff on me. Not for a free gift!"

He leaned over the older man, who sat speechless before such generosity.

"Now's the time to begin watching, Hugh. Watch every step. And when the pinch comes, get your back against my back!"

He straightened, turned, and was gone.

"Is it possible?" breathed the girl. "Is it possible that he can mean it? Gave all of that to us?"

"Look here!" exclaimed her father gruffly. "You've been letting Jack Moon poison you again' Ronicky. But I tell you straight, wild as Ronicky

169

is, his heart is cleaner than the gold in that sack. A pile cleaner! And his little finger is worth more'n all of Jack Moon. Moon? You think he'll let me go now, and live up to his word? Wait and see, girl. Wait and see!"

She caught her breath.

"Then let's go ask him now. Ask him for liberty to start, dad!"

He got to his feet unwillingly.

"It's no good forcing Jack's hand," he said faintly.

"I tell you," insisted the girl, "he's a better man than we dreamed. If he hasn't told me the truth, then there's no truth in any living man! Dad, he means to do all he can for us!"

"That," said her father, "is what you said about Ronicky Doone. And now you've changed your mind."

"Ronicky Doone has some purpose," she insisted. "Jack explained him. He means well enough. He acts on impulse. Just now he has given you gold. In ten minutes he may murder you to get it back again! That's his character — as unstable as wind!"

Her father merely snorted in answer.

"All right," he said. "I'm going to walk right up to Jack and tell him I'm ready to start. And you see what happens!"

She followed at a distance of a few paces. And it was her wide, frightened eyes of which Jack Moon was aware, not the strained face of Hugh himself.

"Jack," said the suppliant, "I've come to ask you to live up to the promise you made. I want to know when I can start home to Trainor."

The answer of the leader was made instantly.

"Any time you want — now, if you say the word!"

It staggered Hugh more than a blunt refusal. He could merely gape at Moon, and the latter was conscious of the flush of happiness which overspread the face of the girl. It was a dangerous game he was playing, and for the sake of bringing that flush into her face it well might be that he was giving her up forever. He went on smoothly enough.

"Blaze away for Trainor this minute if you want, Hugh. They's two things agin' it, but neither of them is me and what I want. You're free as the wind to start, and good luck go with you. But it's a tolerable bad trip in the night, riding through those mountains, and even if you got easy-going hosses you're apt to be plumb tired before you hit Trainor to-morrow. But they's another thing. Hugh" — here his voice lowered and grew gently confidential — "you'd ought to get more'n one share of this stuff. Try to hang on. I'm going to see what can be done for you."

The astonishment of Hugh Dawn was as great as though the ground had opened before his feet. He blinked. He tried to speak.

"You mean —" he began.

"I mean what I say," said Jack Moon, smiling. "If you're in doubt, just ask your daughter. I've

171

told her everything. Now go back to your shack and go to sleep. Main reason being because you need rest, and I aim to get you on your way before sunup. No use letting the rest of the crowd know that you've slipped away. I may decide to tell 'em that you've just given us the slip. But if you want to go now, start — and I'll see that they ain't a hand raised to stop you!"

Hugh Dawn hesitated, then nodded. The dominant tone of the outlaw overwhelmed him.

"You're mostly always right," he admitted, "though it sure strikes me dumb having you thinking on my side of things like this!"

The hand of Moon fell gently on the shoulder of his old follower.

"Partner," he said, "I've been thinking on your side ever since I saw your girl. The father of a girl like that is all right!"

He had allowed his voice to swell as though in the stress of his honest emotion, and from the corner of his eye he studied the effect of his words upon the girl. He was amply rewarded by the shining of her eyes.

"I wanted to throw a scare into you, Hugh. I sure wanted to do that. But I never meant to do any more — after I seen you and the girl together at Cosslett's the other night. Before that I figured you were no good, you see? Just a traitor to me and the crowd and your word of honor. Afterward I seen why you had to leave us, and I didn't much blame you. With a daughter like that to take care of, you'd of been a no-good skunk to of stayed with me. Go back to your shack now, Hugh. Have a sleep. I'll tend to all the rest!"

He struck him lightly and reassuringly on the shoulder as he spoke, and Hugh Dawn flushed with gratitude. After all, his was a hearty nature, and the reaction from his long suspicion of Moon was sudden and violent.

"Jack," he said, in an uneven voice, "I been thinking a lot of hard thoughts about you. I been telling the girl she was a fool to believe you, but I see that you're straight, after all. No matter what you've done to others, you're playing a white game with me, and if a pinch ever comes later on when I can help you, lay to it that I'm your man!"

He shook hands strongly with Moon and turned away.

His daughter swung in beside him with tears bright in her eyes. "I told you," she was saying. "He's a good man at heart, dad, just as I said he was!"

"He's been changed," muttered her father, with great emotion, "and it's you that's done the changing; almost by his account you are, Jerry. And Heaven bless you for it. It's the smile of your mother that you've got, Jerry. And that's what's saved me this time from a dog's death!"

He had picked up his own gold and the share which Ronicky had given him, and under that great weight he walked with slow, short steps toward the shack in which he had spent the preceding night. From the door, where he deposited it, he and Geraldine looked back at the party around the camp fire.

It had been growing wilder and noisier during the past hour. The camp fire had been built up to a comfortable height, so that the heat of it carried even to the shack where the girl and her father stood. It threw, also, a terrible and living light on the faces of the band of Jack Moon where they sat in groups of four, playing cards. Three groups of four, and on the table before each player was a glittering little pile of yellow metal. Usually gambling was a silent and serious effort, but tonight, with raw gold for the stakes, they played like madmen, shouting and calling from table to table. Pounds of gold were wagered on a single hand, and the loser laughed at his losses. For they had seen a fortune taken out of mother earth that day, and, if this were gone, might there not be another hoard some place, discoverable by such lucky fellows as those who followed that prince of leaders, Jack Moon? Such, at least, seemed to be their spirit as they played poker. The unshaven faces grew more and more animal-like as, from the distance, the firelight seemed redder and the shadows blacker than ever.

"They're terrible men," said the girl. "Ah, dad, what if Jack Moon should lose control of them!"

"Him?" The father chuckled confidently. "He'll never lose control. Little you know Jack Moon, girl, if you think that any dozen men can get the upper hand of him!"

"But suppose some of them should lose a great

deal and remember that you have money and —"

"Long as Moon is on our side, we're safe as though we had a thousand. Stop worrying. Go to sleep — and trust in Jack Moon. Fear him when he's agin' you; but trust him like a rock when he's behind you. No, sir, no dozen men can handle him. But if it come to a pinch — I dunno; yonder may be a man that'd give him a hard rub!"

"Where?"

"Close to that pine."

He pointed again, and she made out the form of Ronicky Doone where he stood with his arms folded across his chest, looking on at the games.

"He doesn't play," she remarked.

"He's smelling trouble," said her father, "and that's why he's keeping his nerves steady. If him and the chief meet up, then'll come the big noise and the big trouble, girl. You lay to that! One nacheral fighting man is worse'n a hundred common ones to handle!"

# CHAPTER XX

## BEATEN

As Hugh Dawn disappeared inside his shack, Jerry strolled slowly toward her own hut. She recalled the man who had brought her and her father safely from the house when Moon and his band stole toward it. She recalled the keen face of Ronicky when they worked over the puzzling record through which Cosslett had left trace of his buried treasure. Swift of hand, steady of eye, resourceful of brain — after all, her father might be right, and in the slender figure of Ronicky there might be locked sufficient power to match the big body and the strong brain of Jack Moon. What the eyes told her, was simply an overwhelming contrast; what the memory told her, equaled the scales to some extent. But how could her father speak of Ronicky and Moon as though they were antagonists, when Ronicky was now, it seemed, a member of Moon's own band? Did he mean that the two might battle for supremacy inside the band?

She swerved directly so as to pass close to Ronicky Doone, and she noted that he paid not the slightest heed to her. At that, she paused. He had admired her before, she knew. Perhaps it might have been more than admiration, but now he looked past her into thin space.

"Ronicky!" she murmured, as she paused near him.

His glance turned upon her swiftly, and he nodded; but then his eyes traveled past her again and toward those groups of gamblers, flashing from face to face as though he found the twelve an intricate and dangerous study. Why was that? she wondered.

"I've come to tell you, Ronicky," she went on, "that our troubles are ended. Jack Moon is going to let dad leave in the morning. In fact, we can leave now, if we wish!"

"You can?" cried Ronicky, in such a tone of amazement that she stared at him. "Then — then how quick can you get going?"

"But we're not going to go until the morning."

Ronicky sighed. "I thought not," he muttered. "I s'pose Moon told you it'd be better to wait till there was some light on the trails over the mountains. He's deep!"

"You hate him blindly," insisted the girl. "But that isn't the point. In the morning I may leave without having a chance to see you again. Now that you've taken up this terrible life, I suppose I'll never see you again after to-morrow!"

"I sure take it kind," said Ronicky, but his voice was cold, "that you've wasted any time thinking about that."

"Oh, Ronicky," cried the girl, "I know you're close to hating me for things I've said to you in the last few days, but it's always been because it hurt me to see you go the way you've gone. But to the end of my life, Ronicky, I'll keep hold on my first impression of you, generous and brave, and kinder than any man who has ever come into my life. I want you to know this before I see you for the last time!"

To her surprise, the tribute merely made him smile, and there was no gentleness in his face.

"You ain't seeing me for the last time," he declared. "And — Heaven willing — to-morrow ain't going to be the last day, either. Jack Moon'll see to that."

"You think he doesn't mean what he's promised? That he'll keep us after all?"

Ronicky merely smiled. And she was angered again.

"You hate him," she said fiercely, "merely because you know that he sees through you; and that — that's contemptible! I came here to tell you how sorry I am that you've gone the way you are going — but now I only have to say that I scorn your suspicions — and I scorn you!"

But as she turned away she saw that he still was paying no heed to her but kept his eager, intent gaze fixed upon the gamblers.

The ending of that interview had been marked by Jack Moon, and when he saw the girl toss her head and turn away he smiled with satisfaction. It meant that his most daring scheme had met with perfect success. Only by using Ronicky Doone as a foil had he been able to worm his way into the confidence of the girl. Now he was on the high road to success. That road was a difficult and long one to travel, even now. But much might be done with caution and steady diplomacy. Great problems still confronted him. Hugh Dawn must be disposed of. And terrible Ronicky Doone must be brushed from the way. Most difficult of all, the girl must listen to him when he decided to talk as he had never yet talked to any human being.

There would be time for these things. Meanwhile, the last few minutes had brought about a state of affairs for which he had been watching and waiting.

The gambling had ceased to be a gay and noisy affair. The exuberance of spirits which naturally followed the finding of the gold had gradually died away, and the silence of the gaming hall now brooded over the little groups, each squatted cross-legged about saddle blankets. The winner now dragged in his stakes with a glint of the eye. The loser saw his gold go with a savage out-thrust of the lower jaw.

The losers were more numerous than the winners. Silas Treat had almost cleaned out the entire stakes of his own group. Baldy McNair had well nigh emptied the pockets at another blanket. Indeed, in each group there gradually came to be one corner toward which there was a steady drifting of profits. There was a natural reason. The best gamblers had avoided one another's company, and each had selected a place where he would have a chance for uninterrupted fleecing.

In only one place had things gone amiss, and that was with the most expert gambler of all, Bud Kent. The little bow-legged, broad-shouldered fellow ordinarily was a steady winner, and this night he saw a chance to win, at his own blanket, a hundred thousand dollars in better than cash. So, with glinting eyes, he had settled to his task. But fate, called luck among gamblers, was against him. His three of a kind was invariably topped by a higher three. And once a flush was beaten by a higher flush! When he bluffed, some one was sure to call him. When he nursed the betting cautiously in the beginning to keep from betraying the real strength of his hand, some one was sure to call him, and his winnings were paltry. And at length, plunging his last four pounds of metal on a full house, he lost his final scrap of the treasure and rose from the blanket — broke!

Not a word, not a glance followed him. The remaining three shifted their places a little and closed the gap which he had left, as well-drilled soldiers close the gap where a comrade falls in the charge. Each of the three had shared in the plundering of Bud; each of the three was confident he could keep on winning from his companions. But Kent went gloomily to the leader.

"You seen that?" he said, in a deep voice of disgust.

"I seen it." The chief nodded.

"Can you beat it?"

"Hard luck," said Jack Moon, who knew perfectly what was coming.

"Well, sir," went on Bud Kent, "there lies a hundred thousand in gold, and if I hadn't hit that last streak of bad luck I'd of cleaned the whole thing up. Eh?"

"Maybe you would," said the leader.

"Maybe? I'd of been sure to! Ain't I played with all these gents time and again and always trimmed them? They can't sit in the same game with me. Only the luck held steady for them and steady against me. But a couple more hands would of changed things. Luck? I never seen it hold like this! See that brace of bullets and the three nines I held? And four measly deuces come out and beat me!"

He groaned at the thought.

"If you was to back me," he said suddenly, "I could clean out the whole mess. If you was to back me, I'd split the winnings with you, Jack."

"Thanks," said Jack Moon soberly.

"I'd make it two parts for you and one part for me," persisted Bud Kent.

"I can't do it, Bud," said Moon as kindly as possible. "You know how it is with me. If I backed you, then the next fellow who went busted would come and ask me to back him. And then the next and the next. Of course you and me know that it's different with you. We know that you sure can gamble. But the other boys wouldn't see it that way. They'd think that because I backed you I ought to back them. They'd accuse me of playing favorites. That's clear, ain't it, Bud?"

"But you wouldn't have to say anything," suggested Bud. "Just slip me a handful of the stuff and —"

"They'd know where you got it. Nobody but me would stake any of the boys. If you think I'm wrong, go around to some of the other blankets and ask some of the fellows for a handout. See what you get!"

"I know," grunted Bud Kent, and he rolled his eyes savagely at his former companions. "I'll make 'em pay sooner or later," he declared. "The swine! Not a one in the crowd that'll stake me!"

"What about Hugh Dawn?" suggested the leader.

Bud Kent looked up at him sharply. But Jack Moon, having dropped his sinister suggestion, was staring idly up to the dark of the sky.

# CHAPTER XXI

## MOON IS BAFFLED

The silence continued through a breathless moment.

"D'you mean it?" gasped Bud Kent at last.

"Mean what?" said Jack Moon, and his eye was innocent as the eye of a child.

Bud Kent considered his master. The moods of Jack Moon, he knew, were variable as the moods of the west wind. Other members of the crowd strove, from time to time, to find the meanings hidden in that implacable and cunning mind, but Bud Kent, the oldest member of the crew, had ceased striving to find the clew to the riddle. What Moon thought was his own property, and it was dangerous to attempt to read two meanings into his words. But now Bud scanned the face of the master and hungered for knowledge. What was the significance of that short phrase of a moment ago?

"You think," said Bud at length, very slowly and very cautiously, "that Hugh ain't got much use for his money?"

"I dunno," said the leader, as carelessly as ever. "I ain't asked him about it."

183

"It might take a lot of persuading," said Bud Kent, "and I ain't much at talk."

"Sure you ain't," said the other. "So you better arrange it so's there won't be no need for chatter."

Bud Kent moistened his lips, parted them to speak, changed his mind, and finally managed to whisper: "Chief, talk out. I don't foller you exactly."

"How to stop talk?" replied the leader casually. "Any fool knows that. What mostly keeps a gent from talking?"

"Being persuaded, I guess."

"Think you can persuade a man out of thirty thousand dollars?"

Bud swallowed hard.

"I dunno," he said desperately. "You might stop a gent by gagging him."

He grinned, so that this last suggestion might pass in lieu of a jest if need be. But Jack Moon kept an entirely sober face. All the time he was watching the effect on Bud Kent. He was as interested as the scientist who watches the insect wriggle under the touch of acid.

"Gagging?" said he. "That's a fool idea."

"What is your idea?" asked Bud.

"Look here. I had to promise Dawn his share before I could find out where the gold was, didn't I? And then I gave him the gold, didn't I?"

"Sure."

"But I ain't his guardian, am I? After giving the stuff to him, I don't have to stay up all night to guard it, do I?"

"No, no!" breathed Bud, beginning to see the light.

"It sure ought to be clear to you, Bud, that it don't make me any too happy to see a skunk like Dawn, that's left the crowd once, get away with all that loot."

"That's clear, chief."

"Then, if a gent was to slip in soft to Hugh's hut and grab the coin —"

"With three other men sleeping around him?"

"I'll see that he sleeps alone to-night. They ain't any need of guarding him. He thinks he's extra safe with us now!"

"Ah!" murmured Bud.

"What you want is a stake," went on Jack Moon. "To-night ain't the only night for poker. They'll be another and then another, until the gold is all collected up in the hands of two or three of the boys. Well, Bud, you're soft moving and silent. If you was to slide in and take the stuff, it wouldn't make me extra mad. But mind this: They's no harm to come to Hugh Dawn!"

Bud Kent replied with a broad grin, nodded, and then said suddenly: "But suppose he makes a kick about his money in the morning when he finds it's gone? Suppose they search for it and find it in my saddlebags?"

"If you're enough of a fool not to bury it, son, I suppose they would find it in your saddlebags."

Bud Kent waited to hear no more, but, nodding to his chief with a whispered word of gratitude,

185

he sauntered back to watch the game he had just left.

On and on to midnight the game continued, but by this time the terrific labors of the last two days began to tell. The gold fever was dying out, and, without this stimulant to keep them going, heads began to nod and eyes began to grow filmy. Seymour and Craig by this time were also broke; they joined Bud Kent as a gallery to watch the others. But at length, by mutual consent and almost at the same moment, the games were broken up and the gamblers staggered hollow-eyed toward their shacks. Here Jack Moon, who had been waiting for this moment, assigned them swiftly to their separate lodgings. He kept his promise to Bud, steering the others away from the hut of Dawn. The pretext was easily found — no use waking up a sleeper when there was plenty of room in other huts. One shack for the girl, one for her father, and the other structures afforded room for thrice the whole number of men.

Meanwhile Ronicky waited until the leader was out of sight. Then he glanced about the clearing. Other than himself, every man in the crowd was busy with getting into his blankets — all except the two outposts detailed to keep watch south and north, unfailing precautions which the bandit chief never overlooked. But the clearing itself was the very apotheosis of peace. Not a voice sounded, not a footfall was to be heard. All was dull quiet, and Ronicky turned his back on the scene, entered the hut, and straightened out his own blanket.

One by one the breathing of the men in the hut became more deep and regular. He himself imitated the same sound and lay back, veiling his eyes with the lids and only peering out through the curtain of lashes. The silence grew more and more deep, it seemed to him. The heavier sound of Treat's breathing sounded above the hushed chorus of the others. Some one was snoring in a nearby hut. But beyond and above was the silence.

It was, indeed, too quiet. It was the quiet of a snare, an illusion, a trap. And one of those impulses which no man can really explain, came to Ronicky. An hour had passed since he lay down, and still sleep was far from his eyes. At length, with the softness of a guilty man who dreads oversight, he drew back his blanket and sat up. Finally he rose to a crouching position, stole to the door, and looked out on to the clearing.

# CHAPTER XXII

# TWO AGAINST TWELVE

He saw nothing at first, and he was about to dismiss his foolish fears when something stirred near the hut in which the girl slept. Ronicky Doone was instantly alert. Staring fixedly, he saw the thing again.

It was the form of a man crawling in an almost prone position so that the ground shadows well nigh covered him from the most searching view. Suspicion had been like a searchlight to pick out the figure for Ronicky Doone. Ordinarily, he would never have seen it.

The fellow, whoever he might be, had just crawled out of sight behind the shack of the girl. Ronicky slid back to his blankets, buckled his cartridge belt about him, and, blessing the fact that he had no riding boots to encumber his stockinged feet, he stole again to the door, prepared to stalk toward the hut of Jerry Dawn.

But as he reached the door again, the figure reappeared on the nearer side of the girl's hut and crawled on until it passed behind the next shack, that where Hugh Dawn slept, and, though Ronicky waited an ample time, the stalker did not reappear. Then suddenly it flashed across the mind of the watcher that Hugh Dawn slept alone in that shack this night! Was there some ulterior purpose in the kindly insistence of Moon that Hugh be allowed to sleep on, undisturbed by the coming of others in his shack?

Ronicky did not pause to dissect possibilities. That was not his habit. He was instantly out of the door and going across the clearing at a stealthy pace.

Was it Moon himself who wandered about the camp and spied on Hugh Dawn, fearful lest the man steal away with his share of the gold during the night?

Another moment and Ronicky was crouched just under the wall of the cabin. Slowly, inch by inch — how painful was the movement! — he raised his head and looked into the interior of the shack from the window at the side of the building.

He was right. The stalker had aimed at entering the shack of Dawn, for the back door of the little house was still ajar, and standing framed in it was the figure of the intruder. Hugh Dawn himself lay near the wall, his right arm thrown loosely about the sack which contained his share of Cosslett's plunder.

Ronicky Doone drew his revolver and waited.

The progress of the thief, if that were indeed his purpose, was infinitely slow. His forward glide was hardly faster than the steady drifting of the second hand around the dial of a watch. Presently, he leaned above the sleeper and laid hold on the canvas bag. With a cautious slowness he began to lift the burden.

The straining eyes of Ronicky now enabled him to see more details. When the bag began to be moved, for instance, he saw the hand of Dawn stir, and as it stirred a bright bit of steel was raised and poised in the hand of the thief. Now the bag, however, was safely drawn above the encircling arm of Dawn.

It was the gold itself which betrayed the thief. For as he came on his feet with that burden, the rotten old boards which floored the shack gave under him, and there was a faint squeak as board rubbed against board.

Instantly the sleeper wakened with a gasp that promised to be his last, for the knife flashed up in the hand of the thief. No mistaking that motion. He meant to strike, and he meant to strike home. Ronicky Doone fired.

When he leaped around the corner of the house and sprang through the door, he saw Hugh Dawn standing with a revolver in each hand, while a still form lay on the floor before him. Those two guns jumped up and were leveled against Ronicky.

"Don't shoot!" cried Ronicky. "Light your lantern. Quick, Hugh! Is it Moon?"

And all his heart rose up in hope that it might indeed be the master criminal.

"You, Ronicky?" breathed Dawn. "I might of knowed you'd be the one to keep watch over me tonight when I trusted to Moon's word, like a fool, and figured myself safe. Here's a light. I seen the knife drop in his hand when you shot. Fifth part of another second, and I'd be where he is now!"

His trembling hands ignited a lantern, and as the smoking flame rose Ronicky turned the dead man upon his back. They both looked down into the sullen, relaxed features of Bud Kent. The bullet had struck him in the back of the head and came out again squarely between the eyes, a grisly wound. In falling, the canvas bag had struck the floor beside the victim, and part of the gleaming contents had tumbled beside him. If ever gold had killed a man, here was a sample! Ronicky turned to Hugh Dawn, the latter trembling from the narrowness of his escape.

"Now," he said, "we're in for thunder and battle, Dawn. Guard the house, I'm going to try to get Jerry in here, or otherwise the swine Moon will —"

He stopped, for the sound of clamoring voices broke in upon him. Then there was a rush of running feet and shouting across the clearing and the well-known bass thunder of Jack Moon's voice calling: "Steady, boys, and get back here. I'll do the exploring!"

Ronicky jumped to the front door.

Every man of the band was out in the clearing, and guns gleamed in every hand. Jack Moon was striding toward the shack at a long-gaited run. It was too late to reach Jerry Dawn unless she would come at his call.

"Jerry!" he shouted. "Jerry Dawn!"

And he halted Moon with a clear-ringing warning: "Get back, Moon, or I'll drill you through!"

The bandit stopped as the frightened face of Jerry appeared at the door of her shack.

"Jerry!" called Ronicky Doone. "Come here, quick! Don't stop for nothing!"

"Si!" shouted Moon in counter warning, "get the girl and keep her from that throat-cutter. Jerry, if you trust Ronicky, you trust a man that's just done murder!"

That word was decisive. She shrank back from the door with a cry of terror, and at the same time Silas Treat, who had apparently been running up from the other side of the shack, out of sight of Ronicky, swerved into view for a moment and then sprang into the shack with the girl. Taken by surprise though he was, Ronicky managed to get in a shot, but his aim was so hurried that, even at that short distance, he missed. He was only able to knock the hat from the head of the big man, and the wide sombrero fluttered clumsily toward the ground.

In the meantime, the rest of the band in the clearing had dived for cover, and as they did so they sent a volley which crashed into the solid log walls of the hut about the doorway where Ronicky stood. He himself took to cover, calling to Hugh Dawn to turn down the flame of the lantern so as to give the enemy a dimmer target.

An instant of silence settled over the battlefield.

192

In that breathing space Ronicky turned to his older companion and found Dawn cool and steady as a rock. The time had come for action now, and the big fellow was ready. He had now taken his post in the corner of the shack, covering, in that fashion, both the rear door and the single window to the east, facing the hut which now contained his daughter and Silas Treat.

"Get out of line!" warned Ronicky hastily. "Get out of line, Hugh! They'll be trying pot shots at the window and at the door pretty pronto."

The other nodded and stepped back. And then they heard the wailing voice of Jerry Dawn crying: "Dad! Oh, dad! Are you there? Are you safe?"

He roared the answer: "Safe and sound, girl, thanks to Ronicky Doone! Murder they can call it if they will, but it was Bud Kent or me. Ronicky dropped Bud in time to save my neck. Watch yourself, Jerry, and come to us when you can! You —"

A shouting rose in the clearing, and then a crackle of guns, which Ronicky shrewdly guessed was more to drown the sound of Hugh's voice than in the hope of dropping one of the two.

Then came a frightened cry: "Dad! Help!"

But it was Ronicky Doone who responded to that call.

"They're taking her away from the shack!" he cried to Dawn. "The dogs!"

He started for the door with a fierce murmur, like that of a bull terrier before it springs at the throat of an enemy. Hugh Dawn hurled himself after his companion and gathered the smaller man into the huge embrace of his arms, where Ronicky strove vainly to worm his way toward liberty, writhing and twisting and panting.

"Let me go, Hugh!" he shouted. "Let me get at 'em!"

"You fool!" gasped Dawn. "Don't you know that the minute you show your head it'll be loaded with bullets? And when you go, I go, too! One man can't hold two doors and a window. Ronicky, for both our sakes we got to play safe!"

Ronicky Doone, weak with rage and disappointment, submitted and stood leaning against the wall.

"They've got her," he groaned. "And now they'll ride off with her, Hugh. They've got her and most of the money that Cosslett buried. And now — Heaven knows what'll happen! When I had that chance to fight Moon man to man, why didn't I take it?" He added sadly: "Now I've lost everything!"

"She'll come to no harm in their hands," insisted the girl's father.

"No harm?" said Ronicky. "They won't lay hand on her. I know that. But the main danger is that Moon has a chance to talk to her, the snake! And no one knows what he'll be able to persuade her to!"

"After he's sent a man to murder me? After he's taken her and is keeping her away from me by force? After he's set a siege to the cabin where

194

I am? D'you think he can persuade away all those things?"

"He could persuade the angels that he was one of 'em, if he had a chance," said Ronicky gloomily. "Hush! There's the devil himself calling to us."

"Doone! Ronicky Doone!" called the voice of Jack Moon.

"I hear you," answered Ronicky. "Talk out, Moon."

"Do I get a truce?" said Moon. "If I come out to talk to you, Ronicky, will you and Hugh promise to gimme a chance to get back safe? I want to tell you —"

"Come out," said Ronicky. "You know I won't plug you. I wish I was the kind that would take an advantage. But I ain't your brand of man, Jack Moon!"

Without waiting for a further assurance, Jack Moon appeared across the clearing at the door of the shack facing that of Ronicky and Hugh. He advanced until he was three paces from Ronicky, who remained in the shadow at the door.

"Stop there!" commanded Ronicky. "That's close enough for talk."

"If you don't trust me," said Moon, "right enough! But here I am one man against two, and yet you're afraid."

Ronicky answered indirectly.

"Watch the back of the house, Hugh," he directed, "and watch sharp. If a head or a hand shows, take a potshot. They might try to rush from behind while Moon chats here in front. Now go on and talk, Moon. I suppose you want the body of Kent?"

"Was it Bud Kent you murdered, Ronicky?"

"Murdered? And you mean to say you didn't send him? You didn't send him to knife Hugh and get Hugh's share of the stuff?"

"They ain't no use trying to persuade you different," said the leader gravely, "if you look at it that way. But use sense, Ronicky, and you'll see that it didn't mean anything to me to wipe Hugh out of the way! You know what means more to me than anything else, and that's the good opinion of Jerry. Would I get that if I had her father killed?"

"You'd of talked her into thinking that you didn't send Kent."

"And I didn't!"

"You lie, Moon. I saw you talking to him."

"He was asking me for money. He lost all his share, and he wanted another stake to gamble with. I wouldn't give him anything, and the dog came here to steal. Ronicky — and you, Dawn — I want you to listen to sense. The boys are red-hot for action. They want the scalps of both of you, and if they's any more resistance, they'll get your scalps! But you know the way I stand. I've got to get you off if I can, for the sake of the girl and what she'll think. Boys, if you'll come out with me and give yourselves up and trust me, I can get you scot-free, I think. Otherwise, you're no better'n dead."

"I trusted you once before," said Hugh Dawn, "and near got my gullet opened for it. No more of that, Moon. I ain't a plumb fool!"

"No use trying to argue you out of that," said Moon, "if you've got your mind all set that way. But you'll see how it comes out. The boys'll roast you out of the shack. But that's up to you. Meantime, give me Kent's body, and I'll take it back — and Heaven help you for what's coming!"

Hugh Dawn raised the dead man and gave the burden to the waiting arms of the leader, who now turned his back and trudged slowly away, bearing his grisly load.

Then Dawn turned with a gray face to Ronicky. "I'd forgot the danger of fire," he said. "D'you think he'll use it?"

"He'll use anything, if he can get at us. But we got to wait and see. How much water have we here?"

Hugh Dawn raised his canteen and shook it. There was a sound of water slushing inside the tin.

"One quart," he said.

That was their total supply.

# CHAPTER XXIII

## MOON'S SINCERITY

Covered by the forest, three men watched the hut which was the fortress of Dawn and Ronicky. Eight remained to receive the leader and his burden, Bud Kent's body. Behind the shelter of the shacks which cut them away from the sight and the guns of Ronicky and Dawn, the outlaws stood in a loosely formed circle and stared silently down into the face of Kent. There was no expression of sorrow from those fierce fellows. They had seen too many companions drop before. But there was a universal turning of eyes to the direction of hidden Ronicky and his companion.

Jerry Dawn, her face hidden in her hands, leaned almost fainting against a tree near by, with Silas Treat, her guard, close to her.

"Si," ordered the commander, "take Miss Dawn away. Give her a walk through the trees."

She submitted to Treat's touch, and they disappeared among the forest's shadows.

"Now, boys," said Jack Moon, "you see the luck that's followed us?"

A dead and ominous silence greeted his speech.

198

"Are you set on giving the house a rush?" he asked.

"Why not fire?" suggested the crafty Baldy McNair.

"Why not a torch and a signal fire to call everybody in the mountains this way?" the leader countered, with a sneer.

It was something the others had not thought of. But now Baldy returned on a different tack.

"We can get close to them in the shack that stands alongside of theirs. There won't have to be no forest fire. We can throw burning sticks onto the roof of their house and rout them out that way, and then the rest of us can stand by and plug them when they try to run. Ain't that simple enough?"

"Mighty simple!" again Jack Moon sneered. "Too simple. The logs of that shack are soaked as wet as they can be from the rains of the last week. And there's been too much shade over the house for the rain to get all dried out again. Most you could do would be to start a slow fire smoldering, and we can't wait for a slow fire to eat into that cabin."

The argument seemed unanswerable.

"But," persisted McNair, "we got to do something. Otherwise, we'll be a laughing stock. What's mostly kept us safe all of this time? The fact that nobody knew our faces or what we were like. It was just known that Jack Moon and his band were worse than the devil, and that we couldn't be follered and found. But if gents get to know that we've let two men sift through our fingers, and if those two gents go out and give a description of what we look like and all that, how long d'you think we'll last? Boys, we'll be signing our own death warrant if we let them two go free! They got to die. And they got to die, even if it costs the chief the good liking of that girl yonder!"

"Boys," said Moon, "let's do the wise thing. I ain't going to stay here and waste words talking and arguing with Baldy McNair about his crazy idea that I want the girl. I'm willing to admit that we'd ought to make a final try at the cabin, and we'll attempt to plug the gents that's in it.

"We'll work out a way of getting at it somehow or other, and then we'll try to finish up Doone and Hugh. But I warn you, it ain't going to be any easy job. If we fail, I'm for starting back over the hills as fast as we can travel, carrying the girl with us, as a hostage, and then, after we get a little distance off, I'm for splitting up and each man going for his home. Does that sound like good sense to the rest of you?"

They all had to admit that it was the best plan. To wait to burn wet logs would be foolish. It might take them two days. To attempt to lay a long siege to the hut which sheltered the two enemies, was even more insane. But by a single rush, using weight of sheer numbers, they might do much. Then, as the leader had suggested, the possession of the girl might prove a point of the utmost importance, if they failed to capture the hut; for, while she was in their hands during their flight,

Doone and Hugh, even though they followed, certainly would not dare to call up the powers of the law to run down the outlaw band.

"Baldy," said the leader, "you and the boys put your heads together and lay a plan. I'm going out to get Si Treat. And when I come back I'll go over the scheme with you. We've got to make the plan and try it out before dawn. By daylight we've got to be on our way north!"

Yet the preparations of Jack Moon, considering the fact that he had just arranged for an attack, were most singular. First he slipped around to the rearmost hut of the three which faced the clearing on this side, opposite to the one in which Doone and Hugh were.

Behind this shack he found in the woods the two tall grays which the girl and her father had ridden out onto the trail. Tall and long of limb they were, and in a pinch it would go hard indeed if the common cow ponies of the band could keep pace with the big fellows.

These two horses he saddled, putting the girl's saddle upon one and his own upon the other. But his preparations did not stop there. From the rest of the horses he selected the two which combined the greatest speed and strength. Then, having saddled them, he packed upon them his own three shares of the gold, shares which he had weighed out so cunningly that in reality there was the weight of four, and close to a hundred thousand dollars' worth of the precious metal was included in the double load.

Still he was not content. Slipping into the next shack, unobserved all this time by the grave council which was deliberating on ways and means of attacking the house of Ronicky, he brought forth another load of the gold, the share of what member of the band he could not tell. This burden he divided carefully between the two grays, putting more than two thirds of it in the saddle-bags of the girl. Before he had ended, he had given to each of the four horses a well-apportioned load equal in weight to a very heavy rider. This done, he advanced, leading the four straight into the wood, making what speed he could, because time was infinitely precious — five minutes saved now might mean four horse-loads of gold saved later on.

He advanced until he was far up on the side of the hill, where he tethered the four horses to a tree of conspicuous size, easily located from a distance. Then he turned back, and after a few minutes of search he found the girl and Silas Treat, who, with stolid obedience, had taken her well on into the forest and was now keeping her in a little clearing.

"Go back to the boys," said the leader to Treat, "and tell them that I'm going to dispose of the girl and then follow later on."

"How is it that you can leave the girl off here and come back yourself?" asked Treat curiously.

"I'll manage that," said the leader. "There are lots of ways of managing."

"This?" queried Treat, and with a broad grin

he passed his forefinger across his throat.

It was done with such inhuman complacence that even the hard heart of Jack Moon revolted.

"Maybe that way," he admitted, eager simply to get rid of his gigantic follower and be alone with the girl. "Now get back, Si, and tell the boys to watch sharp, because Ronicky may start a rush. That's his kind. He don't like inaction, and when he starts he'll do enough to keep all of you warm."

Jerry had not made an effort to escape during the conversation while the two men had turned their backs to her. Instead, she sat on a fallen log with her head supported in both hands, and the leader, approaching, had time even in his rush of thoughts, even in his eagerness to get away, to mark the slenderness of the fingers against her hair.

"Jerry!" he called softly.

She raised her head and stared at him blankly. But even now, after all she had seen and heard, there was no sign of hysterical terror about her. From the first, when a crisis came, she had made no outcry, no noisy appeals, but like a man of firm nerve she had waited for events to develop before she made her decisions, before she moved. She was waiting still as she faced the outlaw, and the big man admired her from the bottom of his heart and pitied her for the lie which he was about to tell.

"Jerry," he went on, "I've come to ask you to trust in me another time."

Her answer was a smile, no more, but the smile was of greater import than a thousand words of scorn, contempt, accusation. Moon winced before her, but he went on as smoothly as possible: "Wait till I get through talking before you make up your mind. Jerry, you know my place in the world. You know how I've fought to gain it. You know that up here in the mountains I'm as good as a king, with a kingdom and followers. Well, I've decided to give it all up — for your sake!"

He waited for that point to tell.

But she said: "So you've hemmed in my father. You've set your bloodhounds around him. And any moment, perhaps now, your men are sneaking up to set fire to his hiding place and shoot him as he runs out. You've done that also for my sake, Jack Moon?"

He wondered at her calmness, until he saw that her hands were gripped. In a man such calm would have preceded a fierce attack. He said: "This'll go to show how wrong it is for folks to make up their minds about other gents until they know! Now listen to what's really happened. My boys want to kill, and they want to kill your father. I guess you know that."

She nodded.

"They were so dead set against him that I didn't dare let them see you around while I was talking to 'em. Seeing you would of made 'em think more and more about Hugh and made 'em wilder and wilder to get at him. That's why I sent you away with Si Treat — so's I could have a chance to be alone with 'em and try to make 'em talk sense and see sense. Well, when you were gone, I tried a high hand with 'em. I knew right enough that they could burn out your father and Ronicky like rats out of a hole. But because of you I had to stop 'em. So I piled up the difficulties and made it look bad to try. Anyway, I made 'em change their minds, which I couldn't of done if you'd been there to sort of urge 'em on to get at Hugh. I made 'em promise to get away as soon as they could and follow after me. So they're going to stay behind me and —"

"And you and I?" queried the girl, vaguely groping toward his meaning.

"And you and I, Jerry, won't be on the north road at all! We'll be driving west as fast as the spurs will send the hosses! Ain't it clear, and ain't it a beauty? There was your father and Doone no better'n dead men, and here I've gotten 'em off free and sound!"

It was all clear to her. Suddenly she cried, with a great impulse of thanksgiving: "Heaven bless you for it!"

"Let them bless you," said the outlaw. "Because, except for you, they'd of been finished sure!"

"But you and I ride west, and your men ride north — Jack Moon, does it mean that you've broken away from them, that you never intend to ride with them again, that you've given up your life of crime?"

"It's all according to what you want it to mean."

"Ah," she murmured, "if I could only trust you for half a minute! If I could only be sure of the thoughts that are going on in that wild, cruel mind of yours! Tell me, are you speaking true?"

"Can you ask that?" he said, dodging her swiftly. Then he cried with utter sincerity: "I'd make myself over a thousand times if one shape of me would get a single smile out of you, Jerry. Will you believe that?"

"After what I've seen —"

"You've seen nothing. Neither you nor anybody else has ever seen a thing! My real self is a buried self, girl! And they's only one thing in the world that can make me what I ought to be."

"I think I know what you mean," she said faintly. "And — and in spite of myself I think you mean what you say. Otherwise, how could you dare to leave your men — to betray them in order to ride with me? Because, Jack Moon, if you have left them, if you are speaking the truth to me, there are some of them who will never leave your trail until they have run you down and killed you like a dog! You know that!"

"Ay, if they could run me down. But they can't. That west road I start on is going to swing off to an east road before long, and you and I are going —"

"Back to Trainor?"

He winced, but then he went on glibly: "We're going to follow it wherever you want it to be followed. But the first thing now is for you and me to get onto our hosses and ride as we never rode

206

before. Will you come?"

"I'll come."

"And trust me?"

"What else can I do?"

"Then," cried the outlaw, "I've started a new life."

And, for the first time in his wild life, he meant what he said!

# CHAPTER XXIV

# PREPARATIONS

All unconscious of the fact that their leader, so long trusted, had at last betrayed them, the band of Jack Moon gathered around Silas Treat when the black-bearded giant strode out of the trees and stood before them.

"Where's Moon?" asked one.

"Back with the girl. Going to put her out of the way while we plan to tackle the house. I told him he'd better knife the filly. That's what he'll do."

"You're a fool, Treat," said Baldy McNair, who took greater liberties in his speech and manner than any other in the band. "You're a fool and a swine. But the chief's right. He'll tie up the girl and leave her in the woods. No use having her around when we rush the house. And no use having her so near she can hear any yells. Has he got her far enough back so's she won't hear much?"

"Pretty near," said Si Treat. "Back there in that little clearing up the hill. The trees would cut off most of the noise near the ground from this direction."

"How long'll it take him?"

"Not long, and he says for us to keep right on planning till he shows up."

"We've made our plan. We're going to scatter and rush the shack from all sides at once. The old boy," Baldy went on to explain, "always figures that we ain't got the gumption to do anything or plan anything while he's away. Like as not he's lying back there in the brush and laughing to himself because we sit around and do nothing, with dead Bud Kent lying here to urge us along. Well, boys, let's up and show Jack Moon that with him or without him we can get along. It's time he was showed that, anyway! I say, let's scatter. Best place to start from is the shack beside Ronicky's. Well, let's half of us get in there and the rest scatter out sort of promiscuous and get ready for the run. We'll call in the other gents that are watching now, and then we'll let drive. If them two in the shack ain't got nine lives apiece, we'll salt 'em away and plant 'em under ground. Are you with me?"

There was a grumble of sullen acquiescence in answer, and the eight began to spread swiftly around the edges of the clearing, taking advantage of all shelter of the trees until they should be within short sprinting distance of the shack.

That hut, in the meantime, remained as silent and as black as though the two men who formerly occupied it had long since taken to flight, melting unseen into the forest by mysterious stealth.

As a matter of fact, they had been hard at work during most of the past hour. It was Ronicky who possessed the feverish urge to get out of the confining quarters of the shack and strive to break through the lines of the enemy by a surprise attack. But the sober warnings of his companion deterred him. As Hugh Dawn repeatedly pointed out, they were being watched all the time, no matter how hushed the silence around the clearing might be. They were being watched by eyes that squinted down the deadly length of rifle barrels, and if they left their shelter and the thick log walls which were strong enough to stop a revolver bullet at least, they would certainly go down before they had taken more than two steps from their place of refuge.

Ronicky Doone submitted.

"But it sure galls me," he had remarked through his teeth, "to think of lying here and getting trapped like a rat! It sure galls me, Hugh. I'd rather die ten times fighting in the open than once behind the walls of a cage!"

The other had nodded, and, reaching through the darkness of the shack, he had laid his hand on the shoulder of his young friend and pressed it with a reassuring firmness. Indeed, Hugh was a rock of unperturbed strength during the entire crisis.

"We got the strong position," he kept assuring Ronicky.

"But suppose they rush us? It ain't more'n a couple of jumps to that nearest hut."

"That's right. But a gent can do a pile of shooting while somebody else is taking a couple of steps."

"In the night?"

"That makes it bad, all right. But I don't think they'll rush your guns, Ronicky! We might hang out the lantern after lighting it. That'd give us some light on one side of the house, anyway."

Ronicky merely laughed at the absurdity of the suggestion.

"They'd smash the lantern to bits with a couple of shots."

"Didn't think of that."

"How much oil is in that lantern?" asked Ronicky suddenly.

"It's a big one. About a quart of oil in it, I guess."

"And what's that old mattress in the corner stuffed with?"

"I dunno."

Ronicky crossed the floor and ripped open the small section of mattress which had once served on the corner bunk. An instant later he muttered a low exclamation of satisfaction and came back with a liberal armful of the waste with which the mattress had been stuffed.

"Now lemme have the lantern," he suggested.

It was given him, and to the astonishment of the elder man Ronicky opened the bottom of the tin support and thoroughly wet large portions of the waste with the kerosene.

"And what in Sam Hill," muttered Hugh Dawn, "d'you figure to win by wasting all that oil, son?"

"I'll show you in a minute."

He continued by lighting the lantern and taking off the chimney. Then he turned down the wick, so that there was only a quivering tongue tip of flame visible.

"They's enough oil," he explained, "to keep that lantern going till pretty near morning, if we don't burn it no faster'n that."

"I don't foller you, Ronicky."

"Well," explained the other, "here I put a pile of this oil-soaked stuff in my corner, and there I put a pile of it alongside of you. Suppose they was to start a rush. The first one of us that sees a move gives a yell and instead of shooting grabs up the waste and passes it over the lantern. The minute the oil comes anywhere near that flame it will bust into fire, and we throw the stuff out through the windows. It'll light up everything for a minute or two. It'll make us miss a half second that we could of used for shooting, but it'll also give us a chance to get in three or four aimed shots. I'd rather have one aimed shot than ten chance cracks at shadows."

Hugh Dawn, as the idea struck home to him, gasped with pleasure.

"I been lying here waiting to die," he admitted. "And now I figure that we got a ghost of a chance to keep 'em off. Just a ghost of a chance. But, Ronicky, ghosts can be mighty important things!"

There was another time of silence. The hour was now close to half past four in the morning, or thereabouts, and it was the period of greatest fatigue, when nervous reactions are slower, when the muscles are deadened for lack of sleep, and the mind is sick for weariness. And yet, once or twice at about this time, Ronicky heard humming.

After all, happiness is a comparative thing. Hugh Dawn had felt that he was to be slaughtered without a chance even to fight. The fighting chance was now to him almost as much as the promise of complete safety to most men. Ronicky, listening, wondered and admired.

"Suppose Jerry could look inside here and see you fighting for me, Ronicky. She'd have to change her mind about a couple of things, eh?"

"Not while Moon is there to talk to her. He won't give her a chance to think. The skunk has double crossed me, Hugh. I was a fool ever to listen to him, but I took his word. He swore that if there was trouble coming, he'd never let his crowd jump me. Him and me would fight it out man to man. That's why I come in — like a fool, partner! But here we are, both trapped, and me in no position to help the way I'd be if I was loose out there among the trees!"

"Maybe not, son. And if there was ever a square-shooter, it's you, Ronicky. Look!" Dawn pointed suddenly. "I seen something move behind the trees."

"And me!" answered Ronicky. "I think I hear somebody sneaking beside the other shack and —"

Suddenly he leaped up from his knees with a yell.

"Hugh! They're at us!"

# CHAPTER XXV

# THE ATTACK

Ronicky had seen two low-moving shadows detach themselves from the front of the neighboring shack and start toward the front of his own at full speed, while from the window of the hut a rifleman began blazing away at his window. That hurricane of bullets, one after the other, should have the effect of making it lively for a marksman attempting to shoot from the aperture.

Ronicky scooped up a quantity of the waste and passed it over the lantern. Instantly the flames burst out, fed by the kerosene, and he hurled the armful, with the flames already sweeping back across his shirt, through the window and out into the night. It fell a considerable distance from the wall, and the wind, catching the flames, lifted them high so that all the surroundings were suddenly and brilliantly illumined.

It revealed the sharpshooter at the opposite window. It revealed the two skulkers midway between the fronts of the shacks. It showed, to the rear, three more breaking toward the shack at full speed. But one and all were checked. They yelled with astonishment and fear at this unexpected flood of light, while at the same time reëchoed shouts of rage and fear from the other side of the house proved that Hugh Dawn had carried out his portion of the maneuver with equal success. Ronicky, aiming only at light, gained more than light. He derived the advantage of a surprise attack.

He began shooting — and shooting to kill. Across the room he heard the roaring of Hugh Dawn's gun as the sturdy old warrior began pumping lead from two revolvers at the same time. Very well. He might make a terrific amount of noise, but it was hardly likely that he would do as much execution as this slender, keen-eyed fellow at the window, planting his shots and wasting few of them indeed.

First of all he fired not at the onrushing forms, but directed his attention to the man at the opposite window. For he possessed a rifle, and he could take advantage of the flaring light from the waste, as it burned, to drive home a fatal shot. Straight at him Ronicky drove his first bullet, and he saw the other fling up his arms and sink from sight without a word.

In the meantime, the two men in the front had, after their moment of hesitation on being flooded with light, resumed their forward run, and another stride would take them into shelter around the corner of the hut. One of these Ronicky nailed midstride and saw the fellow pitch to his fate with a shrill scream of pain. But his companion shot out of view behind the corner of the logs.

There would be a future danger, for the man

was now under the wall, and the logs protected him fully as much as they protected the men inside the hut.

Ronicky gave that danger only a fleeting thought. He had whirled, and now he looked to the south, where the three had been sweeping up from the woods.

His first bullet went wild — the sudden change of direction had thrown him off. His second bullet made the middle man of the three stagger and reel, but the ruffian kept on running. His third shot sent the left-hand fellow whirling about, and he dropped on his face. Before he could fire again, both of the survivors of the rush were under the protection of the walls.

At the same instant the firing of Hugh Dawn stopped, and Ronicky wheeled toward his companion.

"How many?" he whispered.

"Nailed one, sure," replied Hugh Dawn, breathing hard. "And you?"

"Three!" murmured Ronicky. "Down, Hugh!"

He followed his own precepts by flattening himself against the floor. Well for him that he did so! Scarcely was he down and Hugh crouched likewise in the far and shadowy corner of the hut, when a shadowy form darted into the open doorway and blazed away at the window where Ronicky had been standing. Too late the outlaw saw the target sprawled along the floor instead of erect, and changed his aim. Before he could get in a second shot Ronicky had fired for the sixth time, and the other, gasping with agony, spun over and disappeared through the doorway and into the outer night.

Then came silence.

"Did you turn 'em?" whispered Ronicky.

"Every one! One down and four went back — and a couple of them, I think, was nicked a little!"

His exultation shook his voice. But Ronicky pointed to the rear of the house with a warning gesture.

Of the eleven men of Moon's band, four had fallen dead, or apparently dead, in the attack. Two had been badly wounded by Ronicky, and perhaps one or more of the others had been struck by the bullets of Hugh Dawn. In a word, where the odds had been, counting Jack Moon, twelve to two, they had suddenly shrunk through this rushing assault and its attendant casualties to the far less imposing total of seven to two. Of the seven, at least two were badly hurt. It left at the most not more than five fighting effectives. But Ronicky, not knowing that Jack Moon had deserted his men, and never dreaming but that he was the directing mind behind the rush, counted the odds still three to one.

The attack had at least placed the outlaws in a superior position to that which they had held before. One wounded man and one man sound in body and limb were now under the rear wall of the shack, sheltered by their nearness to it against gunfire from Ronicky or Dawn. Moreover — an incalculable advantage — they could attack suddenly, and they could overhear any but the most secretly whispered communications of Ronicky and Dawn.

That very nearness, however, suggested to Ronicky the next maneuver.

"Watch that rear wall, Hugh!" he called loudly. "Two of the skunks are behind it and may fire through the logs. Watch it close!"

He added in a sudden whisper at the very ear of his companion: "We've got to get out now, Hugh, or wait here and be stuck like rats in the morning. We got to get out! The only way is to make a break across the clearing. You see? They've got two men right under the rear wall now, and that makes it so's we can't shoot out from the back door. The rest of 'em will come up on that side, and then they'll have us six to two, and we're goners at close range!"

Hugh Dawn nodded.

"Straight across the clearing when I give the word," said Ronicky swiftly, taking command as though it had been agreed to put matters into his hands in the crisis. The older man nodded without a word and set his jaw grimly at the thought of that desperate venture.

Ronicky, meantime, was calmly reloading his revolver, keeping the weapon which he had taken from the holster of Bud Kent as a reserve of ammunition. Hugh Dawn imitated the good example.

The fire from the flaming waste was gradually decreasing. The oil which had made the flare so great had now been well nigh exhausted, and the bad light decreased in proportion; but it was still far too bright to admit of a rush for the safe darkness of the trees. A new and more dangerous expedient came to Ronicky Doone.

"Watch well and keep your nerve," he cautioned Dawn, still in the most guarded whisper. "I'm going to explore!"

So saying, he dropped to his knees and boldly slid out from the front door of the little building and toward its left side. In that direction, as he had noted with a glance, the quantity of ignited waste which Hugh Dawn had thrown through the rear door had been far less than that which he himself had flung out. Accordingly, while that which he himself had tossed out was still blazing, the waste of Hugh Dawn was now a darkening mass of cinders casting hardly any light. In that direction, therefore, he hoped to escape observation.

He stayed close to the wall, wriggling forward slowly and constantly scanning the trees before him in search of the glint of a rifle or revolver raised to shoot. But he caught no such deadly glimmer, and for sound there came only the stifled groaning of the wounded men.

So he came, pushing his revolver before him in extended right hand, to the rear of the house and glanced around the corner. As he had expected, he found two men there. But their condition was not at all what he had anticipated. The one lay on his back with his arms cast out crosswise. Above him knelt the huge body of Silas Treat who was making gestures toward the forest as though silently to encourage his backward comrades to come to his aid in this advanced position.

Perhaps they could not see him; perhaps their nerve was not up to undertaking. At any rate, no one had as yet ventured forth. As for the wounded man, it must be he who had stumbled when Ronicky fired the second time at the group of three; and he was far gone, if not fatally hurt. Not an arm's length away was the immense back of Si Treat, seemingly confident that his closeness to the wall made attack from the house impossible.

Ronicky shoved his revolver against the back of the giant's neck. There was a quiver and then a stiffening in that immense body. Then Silas Treat turned his head slowly and without a sound stared into the face of Ronicky.

Why they were not observed, Ronicky could not tell, unless the rest of the band had now shifted around to the shack from which the first of the assault had been launched.

"Drop your gun!" commanded Ronicky, noting from the corner of his eye that the wounded man made no effort to interfere — perhaps he was swooning, as a matter of fact.

Si Treat obeyed without a word, tossing the gun into the shadows.

"Crawl past me," whispered Ronicky to his captive, "and mind that you go slow so's nobody can see you from the forest. With the first shot that's fired, I sink a chunk of lead into your heart, Si! Now move!"

Without answer Silas Treat began obediently to

work his way around Ronicky, past the corner of the shack, and down its side until at Ronicky's order he turned into the interior of the little house.

"Now get back against that wall," commanded Ronicky, "and keep your hands over your head. That's right. Hugh, get that rope and tie him, and tie him hard. I ought to stick a knife into the skunk, and I will if he don't talk out!"

Hugh Dawn, muttering in his astonishment, obeyed and bound their formidable captive tightly. Si Treat, in the meantime, retained an immobile expression, as they could see by the last glimmer of the burning waste.

"Now," said Ronicky, "talk fast and talk straight. Part of what I'm going to ask you I already know. If I catch you in a lie, it's the last word you speak. Understand?"

Treat nodded.

"First: where's the rest of 'em?"

"Gone blind," said the big man savagely, "or else you'd be dead sure, Doone! But they're gone blind. Most like they've sneaked back in the trees to tie up some little cut places where they got nicked. They ain't got the nerve of Baldy McNair. He kept coming after he was drilled for fair."

"That's Baldy lying behind the house?"

"That's him."

"Are any of 'em in the shack next to us here?"

"Nope. Not a soul, unless they sneaked there, and I didn't see 'em. But they won't come that close. They're licked! The yaller dogs! They're licked, or they'd of follered me, and then we'd of had you!"

"Maybe," said Ronicky, stumbling in his haste to get at the desired information, "but where's Jack Moon? Did he go down?"

"Moon? I dunno where he is. Maybe he's deserted. I left him in that little clearing up the hill with the girl. Maybe he's run off with her. He ain't showed up since we started the party."

Ronicky Doone groaned.

"Gone off with Jerry?"

Hugh Dawn inhaled audibly. "It's a lie!" he cried.

"Look here," said Silas Treat, in the same singular calm, "I ain't got any call for lying or playing in with the rest of them swine outside. I done my part. They didn't do theirs. I'm through with 'em. All the good ones are done for, anyway, and Moon's band is busted up. Kent and Bush are dead. Corrigan's dead. Craig is dead and others along with him, and Baldy McNair is lying on his back nearer death than living. Moon's band is busted up, and Moon himself has beat it off with a piece of calico. I'll never trust or foller another man so long's I live!"

"Gag him!" commanded Ronicky. "Gag him so's he can't yell. Hugh, we got to make our break, and we got to make it now. First: Where's the hosses?"

"Over in the woods behind the third shack."

"Any of 'em saddled?"

"Three or four, I guess."

"That's all!"

# CHAPTER XXVI

## ESCAPE

At the word Dawn clapped the gag, which he had meantime improvised, between the teeth of the captive and secured it firmly.

"Now," said Ronicky, "run for it!"

And he darted through the door, followed at his heels by the older man. Half the distance to the trees they had covered with flying haste when there was a yell behind them — a yell from Silas Treat, who had so quickly worked out the gag that silenced him. Then — he must have burst the cords that held him by an exertion of his tremendous strength and scooped up a fallen revolver — a storm of bullets was driven after the fugitives.

But the distance was great, and Ronicky set the example of dodging from side to side as he ran. In a moment, though, the bullets still whistling and crashing through the boughs around them, Ronicky had reached the safety of the forest and turned panting to Dawn.

"Safe?" he asked.

"Thank Heaven! And you, Ronicky?"

"Make for the hosses. Get two and come back.

I'll keep 'em dancing to our music while you get 'em!"

Dawn disappeared, and Ronicky faced the enemy. There was a new confusion of shouts. The enormous voice of Silas Treat was giving directions. The rest of Moon's shattered crew was coming to the firing line, and a scattering of shots was pumped toward the place where Ronicky had disappeared. He must give them the opinion that he and Dawn were preparing to make at least a short stand in this direction. Accordingly, he began to run from tree to tree, firing two shots in quick succession and then two more from another place, so as to give the effect of a pair of fighters working along the edge of the forest. He was aiming at the flashes on the far side of the clearing, but he had no hope of striking a target, and he was not surprised when no cries of pain greeted his attack. In a moment they would send a couple of men sifting around the edge of the clearing to make a flank attack, but now came Hugh Dawn leading one horse and riding another. One bound carried Ronicky into the saddle, and he and Dawn spurred recklessly into the heart of the woods.

Behind them rose fresh yells of dismay, and the firing ceased. Of course they would pursue, but unless Ronicky were hugely mistaken, they would not pursue far through the darkness of the woods. Dawn was indeed beginning in the east, but the pines were thick enough to shut out the scattered rays of light and leave deep night beneath the lower branches.

And to follow an armed enemy who had proved the sharpness of his teeth through such a thicket as this, would probably overtask the worn nerves of the outlaws. Besides, he shrewdly guessed that they had had enough of fighting to last them for many days.

Another interest was larger in the mind of Ronicky. He plunged with Hugh Dawn straight up the slope until he came to the clearing where Treat had said Jack Moon had last gone with the girl.

It was quite empty, as he broke into the open space with his revolver poised. Drawing up his horse with a groan, he cried to Dawn: "Treat was right. The devil has taken Jerry."

"Ay," said the despairing father, "devil he is and doubly a devil, but we'll never get him to-night, Ronicky. He's taken the grays. I seen that they weren't among the rest of the hosses, though I looked for 'em. On the grays he'll shake his heels in our faces, lad, or the faces of any hosses in these parts. They've got the foot. We can't catch 'em!"

For answer Ronicky looked a moment in silence at his companion and then whistled a peculiarly high and piercing note, long held. Then he sat with his head canted a little to one side, listening intently.

"How come?" growled Hugh Dawn uneasily. "Calling up Moon's gang of cutthroats?"

But far away, faint as a small echo, the answer came in the form of a neigh. Ronicky smiled and shook his head at his companion.

"You hear?"

"It's Lou," said the other, a little awed. "She's like a man for sense, Ronicky."

"Better'n most men," answered Ronicky tersely and whistled again.

The answer this time was much closer. Then they heard a crashing in the underbrush, and the beautiful mare came like a bullet out of the trees and glinted in the dawnlight of the clearing. Beside Ronicky she drew up, snorting her pleasure at the reunion.

A change of saddles was quickly made, and now, on the back of the mare, Ronicky laughed with joy.

"Now let Jack Moon ride hard," he said, "because, no matter how much foot the grays have, I'm going to run 'em into the ground — if I can ever pick up the trail. But Lord knows where they've gone. Can you guess, Hugh?"

"Can't make a good guess," the older man returned, watching with an appreciative eye while the bay mare danced in her eagerness to be off. "But how'm I to keep up with that little streak of lightning you're on now?"

"You won't keep up," answered Ronicky. "Never come across a hoss in the mountains that could keep up, partner."

Now the gray morning was brightening each moment, and already the light was so clear that they could look back into the heart of the hollow and see the clearing and the shacks. There was no pursuit apparently. Small figures of men moved here and there hurriedly. There was a knot of horses, looking as small as ants in the distance, in the central space.

"I knew," muttered Ronicky Doone, "that there was a curse on that treasure of Cosslett's. We ain't the men that dug the stuff out of the ground in the first place, and neither did they give it to us. Hugh, they's going to be a curse wherever that gold travels!"

"I got none of it," said Hugh Dawn almost cheerfully. "Left it all behind in the shack. And I think you're right, Ronicky. But now where do we head?"

"We can only guess. Where would a smart gent like Jack Moon go if he wanted to throw folks off the trail?"

"North was where he and the band expected to head."

"That's why he won't head there. And over to the east the ground slopes too easy and smooth. That's where folks would naturally think that Moon had gone trying to get away. But most like, just to throw us off, Moon has taken the west road, through those hills. The harder the road, the less chance we'd have to foller him on it. Ain't that the way he'd think?"

"I dunno, Ronicky. But it sounds pretty reasonable, except that for my part I'd take the east road. That's where he must of gone."

227

"Take it if you want. I go west."

"Take it, then. We'll each try a road. And if we both miss?"

"I'll see you in Trainor — if I come through alive."

"Good-by, Ronicky — and Heaven bless you!"

Ronicky Doone waved his hand cheerfully.

"You look happy," said the older man curiously, "like you was going to a party, son!"

"I am," said Ronicky Doone. "I'm going on the trail of the gent I'd rather meet than anybody in the world. Good luck, Hugh!"

Hugh Dawn waved again and then watched Ronicky send his mare at a gallop down through the sparsely wooded slope leading toward the west. He kept on watching as the rider disappeared in the thicket in the lower hollow, and until Ronicky came into view again on the farther slope. He was still allowing Lou to keep a swift pace, and he was riding jauntily erect, as though he rode to a feast.

Then Hugh Dawn turned his face east and trotted down through the trees.

# CHAPTER XXVII

## THE THREAT

It was, indeed, down the western trail taken by Ronicky, that Jack Moon had urged his horses with Jerry Dawn at his side, and never before had the leader ridden with such high hopes of great success to lure him on. The weariness of the girl was a great part in his favor. He had well nigh convinced her of the honesty of his intentions during the first part of the ride, and now, as the long strain of anxiety and of physical effort during the past few days began to tell upon her, she turned to the strong man beside her automatically for assistance and guidance. If she had been in full possession of her natural keenness, she might have probed motives and probabilities far more deeply. But as it was, she took for granted, it seemed, in the mental fog that springs out of physical exhaustion, that Jack Moon was a rock of support.

She had ceased riding erect and lightly in the saddle by the time the sun pushed up out of the eastern trees and looked down at them as they twisted along a narrow trail on a mountainside. Now her head had lowered a little, and one hand rested heavily on the pommel of the saddle. Sometimes he thought that she was on the verge of falling asleep, so heavily she swung to one side or another as the big gray turned a sharp corner of the trail, but these swerves always wakened her a little and made her smile at her companion with dim amusement. The outlaw pressed close to her side to make sure that she should not fall.

In all his dark and cruel career he had never come so close to a good and pure emotion as he had come now. To him the girl in her weariness and helplessness was a more controlling power than a hundred men with guns rushing at him. The night of sleeplessness, with other dreary nights of watching before, had robbed her of all sprightliness of mind, all elasticity of body. She had become, mentally and physically, a child. He could mold her as he would. Should he take advantage of her now, to press on her the great desire which had been beating at his brain since he first saw her those few short days before?

Watching her wavering in the saddle, he decided that for very shame he could not trouble her with his importunities. But looking more closely again, and this time at her bowed face, it seemed to Jack Moon that there was nothing in the world so tender or so perfectly beautiful as the line of her profile, curving over brow and nose and lips and chin and rounded throat. Behind all the gentleness, he knew there was more courage than ordinarily comes to the lot of woman. All in all, it seemed to him that he had at last found a helpmate — the woman he wished to make his wife.

It must be said in justice to the man that in his associations with women he had ever played an honorable rôle. Whatever his ways with men, he had kept his trickery for them alone, and he had reserved for womankind as much reverence as he possessed. He was one of those odd fellows who, in the midst of a thousand crimes, retain a measure of self-respect by adhering to standards of one kind or another. It is not an unusual characteristic of criminals. There are murderers who kill for a price, and a cheap price, at that, who would scorn to commit an act of thievery. There are robbers who would not keep themselves from starving by descending to such a pitifully small act as picking a pocket. But with Jack Moon the exception had been a very large one — he had built a solid reputation as a man who never broke his word.

He writhed with shame and anguish of spirit to think that at last he had shattered the painfully acquired repute. He had betrayed his own followers, he had tricked and betrayed Ronicky Doone, he had betrayed Hugh Dawn. But he had lied and perjured himself for the sake of the girl, and he had the price of his sin with him. At least he had her presence. How far he was from having won her confidence, her affection, remained to be seen. In the meantime, she was here beside him, and as the miser, looking at his gold, makes small the privations he has endured to heap up the money, so Jack Moon, looking at the girl, sneered at the lost honor which she had cost him.

Yet, how much of her was his? How truly did she trust him? Might it not be that he had paid the terrible price simply for the sake of a single ride with her? All of these possibilities swarmed through the tormented mind of the outlaw, but he forced them away. It was too much to be considered. Never before had he laid siege to the mind of a man without eventually winning him over, and surely a single, weak woman could not endure against his persuasiveness!

But before she could even listen to him, she must be stimulated to complete wakefulness. He halted his party, helped the girl dismount, and built a camp fire hastily. Over it he made coffee, finding all the materials necessary in the pack which was behind the saddle on Jerry's horse. Having prepared a steaming cup of the coffee, he gave it to the girl. Bacon and cracker sandwiches completed the meal, but they both ate ravenously; and before the brief repast was ended, the color was coming back into the face of the girl. Still he did not begin his talk, but waited until they were once more on the trail.

Of course there was not a chance in a thousand that he would be pursued; not a chance, unless Ronicky Doone escaped from the band — which was absurd — and then was able to guess what trail the fugitive leader had taken. But there was not a single danger in a thousand possibilities that Ronicky Doone, if he escaped from the besieged shack, would even be able to guess that the leader of the outlaws was a fugitive! Still Jack Moon preferred to make surety doubly sure. So he pressed steadily westward. Before long they would come down into the lowlands; they would begin to enter a district where the plain was green with irrigation, and where little agricultural villages were dotting the green here and there. In one of these, if his persuasions took effect, he could find the minister. In one of these the ceremony could be performed.

Still he delayed beginning the talk. It was hard to find the right opening. His heartbeat began to quicken; and he could have blessed her when she said suddenly: "It's all like a happy dream, you know. We've been through a nightmare time; it's unreal. I've been trying to convince myself that I've actually seen Cosslett's gold, but I can't."

"And yet we have four horses here, all loaded with it! More than a hundred thousand dollars, Jerry!"

"I wish it weren't here!" she answered. "There's no luck about it."

"If you want," he answered, "I'll pitch the gold down into that ravine and let it lie there. Just say the word!"

The violence of his expression made her glance up to his face, startled; she glanced away as quickly. Such talk as this could mean only one thing. Moreover, she had seen a pale, intense face and eyes that burned out of it at her. The usual pale calm was gone from Jack Moon. He was no longer the aloof, superior leader. He was simply a man, a man in love. She was frightened, but she was not altogether displeased. She cast about, however, for some other topic to carry the talk away from the danger point.

"Perhaps you should. I don't know. Perhaps Ronicky was right."

Moon, gritting his teeth, saw that he must not take up the subject. Apparently the girl had recovered from her former aversion to Ronicky.

"Doone is all right," he said mildly. "Anyway, he stuck by your father in the last pinch."

"I don't know what to make of it," she murmured. "First he seems to throw his own life away, fighting for us against you and your men. He does it for nothing — without a hope of reward. Then he sells his honor and becomes one of your band. Next he leaves the band and at the last moment throws himself on the side of my father again. How do you explain him?"

"I don't try to," said the leader carelessly, far more carelessly than he really wished to speak. "He's just a wild man. That's all! Some gents are all straight and sane about most things, but go off on one subject. That's the way with Doone. Talks straight till he gets a chance to fight. Then he goes mad.

"There's only one thing I'm sorry about," went on Moon, changing the subject, "and that's the gold. I promised to get all of it for your father. But all I can give him is the stuff we have with us."

"You're going to give that to him?"

"Do you think I'm carrying it for my own use?" asked the bandit sorrowfully.

That won him a smile of gratitude.

"I knew you were brave," she said, "and I knew you could be gentle and kind, but I didn't know that you could be so generous."

"It's not for my sake or for his," answered Jack Moon. "It's you that have taught me what to do."

He had come close to the point now, and he must press on.

"Will you let me tell you what I've been planning?"

She knew well enough what direction he was taking now, yet she could not stop him.

"I'm going East," said Jack Moon. "You might think that that's a fool play to make. But mighty few people have ever seen my face. And them that have, would never know me when I'm dressed up in store clothes and wearing gloves and talking smooth. I can put on smooth talk well enough, and lay off on the bum grammar, too, Jerry. You trust to that! So what's to keep me from popping up in the East — in New York, say, with a new name and plenty of money to start me off in business of some kind? What's to stop me from all of that?"

"Nothing," said the girl heartily. "I wish you joy with all my heart. I know you can win out. Nobody would trail you there."

"Nobody," echoed Jack Moon. "And by the same way that I've made a place for myself in the mountains, I'll make a place for myself in business, and I'll make money for myself, too. It won't be hard!"

"No," agreed the girl. "You were born to lead men, Jack, and you can lead them in cities as well as you can in the mountains!"

"Yet," said Jack Moon, "all the money in the world, tied up with a life in a city, wouldn't make up for the freedom I have in the mountains. Up here I'm a king. Down there I'll be just lost in the crowd. You see?"

She nodded, dreading what was to come.

"But there's one thing that would make me go — one thing that would lead me anywhere, Jerry, and that's you! Understand? You, Jerry!"

He swerved his horse close to her and rode with his left hand on the cantle of her saddle. He was leaning so that, when she looked up to him, his tensed face was hardly an inch away. Jerry Dawn grew pale. His words came in a stream now.

"Since I met you, Jerry, I've wanted one thing in the world more than all the rest of it, and that's you. I've quit the band, to follow you. I've given up what it's taken me years to build, to follow you. Understand? I'm through with the mountains — I'm through with the men. I've given it up for a new life, and the heart of the new life is you, Jerry. Without you, it's nothing to me. With you, it's everything. You're getting pale, honey, but it's not because you're afraid. You're too steady to do that. You know that, whatever I've been to the rest of the world, you can trust me to the finish. Will you tell me that, Jerry? Look up and tell me that!"

She flushed, frightened and miserable.

"But don't you see, Jack, that I can only answer you — honestly — in one way, if I answer yes to all that?"

"What way?"

"I can only say that I care for you as you care for me. I — I don't, Jack."

"You couldn't," went on Moon. "It ain't possible that you could. I don't expect you to — yet. But with time, Jerry, I'll pour so much love around you that you can't help giving some of it back, any more than a mirror can help shining back some firelight! Will you believe that, or d'you see me only as an outlaw talking crazy words that mean nothing?"

"Whatever you may have been," she answered, "I tell you truly now that you've honored me by saying all this to me. But, what can I do? I simply don't care for you in that way, Jack. I know that I owe the life of my father to you, and still —"

"Jerry," he implored her, "think it over. Think quick and hard. If you turn me down, I go back where I started. I build a new band. I run the mountains again. But if you say the word, I'll leave the hills. I'll go to the city. I'll work to make you a home and happiness as no other man ever worked for a woman."

Sincerity was in his voice and in his heart. The very fact that she was repulsing him made her the more desirable to Jack Moon. It seemed to him then that the cool gray eyes and the pale, trembling lips of the girl were worth more to him than ten thousand treasures as rich as the treasure of Cosslett.

"I can't answer you in any other way," answered Jerry.

"Is there somebody else?" he said through his teeth.

"Nobody."

"It's that smooth-faced, smiling, good-looking Ronicky Doone?"

"On my honor, there's no one!"

"Then, Jerry, the fact that you don't love me as much as I do you is just nothing! I can't expect you to. But in time I'll teach you how. It takes time for all great things. I'll surround you with it like a wall. You'll know nothing else. Look here. I know what it is to run men. It's better than running a thousand horses to run one man. And me, Jerry — I've run men and run 'em by the scores; and wherever I go, I'll still run men!"

He raised his great head, and his voice swelled.

"Wherever I've gone, I've been king," he declared. "I've never met a man that could match me if it came to strength of muscles or strength of quick thinking. I've planned better than the others, and I've beat 'em in cunning and in tricks. I've read their minds and beat them always. Just the same way, when it come to fighting, I've beat 'em at fighting. I'm going to go East, Jerry, if you say the word, and do the same thing there that I've done in the West. I'm going to run men — run 'em by the score — have 'em working for me! And you, Jerry — you'll be the power behind. You'll be the rider with your hand on the reins. I'll run scores, and you'll run me. You'll be like a queen on a throne, Jerry. You hear?"

She believed him, as she had reason to. It was within his capabilities to do as he said — to build up a power relentlessly strong, to make her rich, to pour treasures into her lap. Wherever he went, he would be king, and she, by very virtue of the fact that she did not love him blindly, could be absolute dictator in his life and carry the great power of the man in the palm of her hand to do with it as she pleased.

Yet she shook her head, though she paused a moment before she answered. It had been a great temptation. Moreover, she knew that the man would lead as straight a life, for her sake, as he had led a criminal one for his own sake.

"I can't do it," she said simply. "I tell you frankly, Jack, that I admire you for your strength, and I'm grateful with all my soul for what you've done for me. But I respect you too much, and I respect all the possibilities in you too much, to do what you ask. There's no use talking any further!"

It was her calmness that laid the whip on him more than her words. He had debased himself before her. He had offered to sell himself. He had, so to speak, put a saddle on his back and offered to go where she bid him, and her refusal tortured him.

"Then," he said suddenly, "Heaven help Hugh Dawn!"

She winced and stared at him.

"I say it again," said the outlaw. "Heaven help Hugh Dawn!"

# CHAPTER XXVIII

## THE LAST CARD

There was no question about the threat which his words implied. He had drawn away from her as he spoke, and now he sat gloomily, drawing his horse to a halt.

"Here's where I leave you," said Jack Moon. "You go on with the hosses, and you take the gold. I've promised you that, and I keep my promise."

"Do you think I value the money a straw's weight?" she cried in terror. "Jack, what do you mean about my father?"

"Why, Jerry," he said, frowning in wonder that she did not understand, "you see there ain't more'n two ways open to me. Either I sell myself out to you and go East as your husband, or else I go back up the north trail and meet my boys and take command again. I'll have to find an explanation for being away so long, but I'll explain it away, right enough, and take command; and, once back in command, I'll forget about you as though you never existed!"

"But my father?"

"Why, the boys have a claim on his life — and he's got to go! He owes us a debt, and he's got

241

to pay. I've busted too many rules already. Once back at the head of the band, I play the game."

"You can't do it," breathed the girl. "You can't do it!"

"You think so?" he answered, almost sneering. "You don't know me, Jerry. There's one thing I love more than the rest of the world, and that's you; but next to you I love power, and to me power is the band. The way I hold the band together is by being as cold as iron and as hard as iron. I rule 'em with a stiff rod, and they come to me when I tell 'em to come, they go when I tell 'em to go. One sign of softening, and they'll turn and sink their teeth in me. So I won't soften!"

It was a bluff. He knew that he had already hopelessly lost the band. But it was a bluff which must win.

"If I don't soften, I've got to get your father out of the way. His life is a forfeit. And it's got to be paid down. I go back up the north trail. I find the boys and swing 'em southward. Before night I ride down your father on the way to Trainor and leave him dead on the trail. There's nothing else to do."

He turned his horse, waving to her, settled his hat more firmly on his head, and touched the gray with the spurs, but at the first leap he heard her voice calling faintly after him. He checked the gray and turned, his heart bounding with triumph.

There she sat with her eyes almost closed in the pain of what she was to do, and both her hands clutched hard over the pommel of the saddle.

"Come back to me," said Jerry Dawn sadly. "I didn't know it was possible. Even now I'd go down on my knees and beg with you, Jack Moon, except that I know it's worse than useless! You are what you say — hard as iron. I surrender. Tell me what I have to do. I'll do it. But I never will forgive you."

A strange sound of choked triumph came from the throat of the outlaw. He had played his last card, to be sure, but that last card had been enough, and he had won. He forbore, however, from pressing his triumph on her.

"We'll ride out of the hills and down into the valley," he said quietly. "And there we'll find a minister in the first town. In that town we'll be married. You understand, Jerry?"

She swallowed and then nodded, never looking at him.

"But when we're East, Jerry, I'll teach you to forgive me. This thing may be hard for you to do. But some day —"

She raised a hand in mute entreaty, and he stopped abruptly. So they rode on in silence until they reached the crest of the highest mountain, where the trail drove straight down before them. Far away, beyond the foothills, stretched the green fields of that rich farming country, and he could see the windows of the first town gleaming faintly in the early rays of the morning sun. There was, indeed, his promised land!

There was a sound of a caught breath from the girl. He glanced aside at her and saw that she had turned in the saddle and was looking back, though when he turned to her she instantly righted herself in the saddle and faced forward again. But that stifled exclamation of pleasure, or fear, aroused his interest, and, searching the ranges of hills which stretched behind and below him in wave after wave, he saw, two crests away, the form of a horseman riding over a summit at full gallop.

The outlaw set his teeth and whipped out the field glasses from the saddle pocket. By the time he had focused the glasses, he was able to catch only a glimpse as the horseman dipped out of sight among the trees, but that glimpse had been enough. He had made out the flashing sides of a bay horse. He had marked the gait of the animal, long and free as the flight of a swallow, dipping lightly up and down on the wind. There was no other horse in the range of the mountains with that high-headed grace, that spiritlike ease of gait. It was the mare, Lou, and that rider was Ronicky Doone!

"Ride!" he called to the girl. "Ride hard, Jerry. Don't put your hopes in the fool behind us. He's late. He's too late, like all the rest that come up against Jack Moon. He's late, and he's beaten!"

"Who is it?" cried the girl above the roar of the hoofs as the horses broke down the slope of the mountain.

"Nobody worth thinking about," said the other. "A gent I could wait for and salt away with lead. But I ain't going to stain our first ride together."

He saw a fleeting sneer cross her face, and the

expression was to him like a blow. Then: "It's Ronicky Doone!" she cried. "Ah, Heaven bless him! It's Ronicky Doone, and you're running from him like a coward. Running from one man like a coward!"

She was even more clever than he had suspected. But after all it was a childish ruse to attempt to badger him into pausing to vindicate his prowess in single combat, while she, perhaps in the midst of the battle, slipped away to safety and rode to warn her father that the devil himself was on their trails! No, Jack Moon merely smiled to himself. Let her show her teeth now. Later on he would teach her what discipline meant! As they spurred on, he noticed that her expression was rather thoughtful than sullen, rather studious than terrified.

They came off the first long down slope of the mountain, and they began to climb the slope of the hill beyond, only a short rise before they would again have a declining grade to make their way the easier and the swifter. Here the girl fell a little behind, but still he could hear her speaking to the horse to urge it on.

Then he heard the grunt of a horse brought to a halt, or wrenched away in a new direction. He turned in haste. Jerry Dawn had whirled the tall gray and was dashing back down the trail as fast as the spurs would drive her mount, and the lead rope which had been bringing the horse on was dangling in the air where she had severed it with a single slash of her knife.

# CHAPTER XXIX

# A VITAL BLOW

The outlaw jerked loose the knot which bound him to his own lead horse, swinging his gray about at the same time, and so he was off in pursuit, his teeth set, and one of those red rages which occasionally swept over him now blurring his eyes. She had reached the long upslope of the mountain while he was still coming down from the hill, so that he gained with tremendous bounds on her; but now she was reaching into the saddlebags and throwing out the treasure of gold which weighted her horse. It fell on the grass and gleamed there, unregarded. What was gold, save a heavy metal, a worse than useless thing to her?

Cursing bitterly, the leader saw the horse of the girl pull away, thus lightened, and he followed the example, hurling out what was in his own saddlebags. Then he bent himself to the serious work of the pursuit.

She was not a dozen feet away. With a lariat he could have roped her horse and brought it to a halt, but there was no rope on his saddle, and he groaned because of the lack. With all his skill brought to bear on the problem, with merciless spurs urging on his mount, he tore after her, but, to favor her horse, she was a full seventy pounds lighter than her gigantic pursuer, and she rode with all the energy she could bring to bear.

No matter how he swung himself with the gallop of his gray, still her mount drew away little by little, widening the gap between them. For they were going up a steep grade, and her weight told as it would never have done on the level; all of the outlaw's skill in the saddle was wasted. He could not gain, he could not keep even with the fugitive. He saw her turn her head and then shout with joyous triumph!

It was worse than merely being distanced. In that merciless drive at full speed up the side of the hill they were burning up precious strength, and the grays would be far from the horses they had been before the spur was started. With spurs, with beating quirt, he drove his gray until he heard the breath of the honest beast come in great, wheezing gasps — and still the other gained, for the girl was whipping as fiercely as himself.

There was nothing else for it. To continue that stern chase was simply to waste valuable time. Moon drew his revolver and poised it. Perhaps bluff, which had won for him before, would win again.

"Jerry!" he shouted. "Stop or I'll shoot."

She turned toward him, and he glimpsed the white, set face.

"I swear it!" called Jack Moon. "I'll shoot unless you stop."

But she merely raised her clenched fist and shook it back at him in hatred and defiance. And suddenly he loved her more than he had ever loved her before. Here, indeed, in this fearless girl, was a mate for him! But could he let her go? Yonder, once over the crest of the hill, she would have downslope to give her horse impetus, and they would be driving straight into the arms of Ronicky Doone. No, he decided fiercely, it was better, far better, to see her die than to let that chance come to him. He aimed with all the skill at his command at the right off hind leg of the fleeing gray and fired. In response there was only a greater burst of speed, and a streak of crimson leaped out on the hip of the wounded horse.

Once more he fired, taking still more careful aim, and this time his bullet struck. The gray pitched up with a snort of pain; then his quarters crumbled beneath him as he strove to take the next driving stride uphill. He sank to the right, and he fell heavily, the girl being flung out of the saddle and turning twice over and over before she struck.

She lay where she dropped, a queerly twisted body with outflung arms, and Jack Moon felt in his heart that she was dead. He was out of the stirrups in an instant and beside her, lifting her in his arms. There was a long gash in her forehead, but it was only a shallow flesh wound where the edge of a sharp rock had clipped the skin. For the rest, as he ran his swift hands over her body, he could feel no broken bones.

Jerry was still alive, she was still with him. Though they had wasted priceless time and burned up the strength of one horse and destroyed another, there was still, perhaps, a fighting chance.

The girl was not badly injured — merely stunned, it seemed; but the cut on her face was flowing. He whipped out his bandanna and knotted it as a crimson bandage about her head. Then he picked her up lightly, as though she had been a child, and ran back to the gray. Once more in the saddle, he spurred back along the hill, heading toward the two led horses. They must be his last resource now — and a bad one to mate against the speed and great-hearted courage of the bay mare, Lou.

But in the meantime, here was the girl, for one moment at least, his. No matter that she was unconscious, for when her senses returned she would either weep or moan her despair. Only for this instant, as the gray bore them with staggering gallop down the hill and the wind whipped into his face, she was his beyond question. Gathering her close to him, he cupped her head in his free hand and kissed her lips.

By the time he reached the led horses and drew up his own mount, the gray was broken of wind and trembling of limb. That burst up the hill had completely shattered his running powers, and he would not be good for an hour more of going such as lay before them. Therefore, he was less than nothing to Jack Moon.

Instead, the outlaw intended to use the two remaining horses. Into one saddle he raised the girl. Into the other he cast himself; first emptying the gold from the pouches along the saddles, he sent the horses ahead at a reckless gallop. The girl, since he could no longer trust her for an instant, he allowed to sit motionless in her saddle; taking the reins of her mount, he urged on both horses.

Truly, the girl had worked better than she knew. She had not delayed them in actual time more than ten minutes, but in fact the delay would prove a far more vital thing. Instead of the ground-devouring swing of the grays there was now the choppy stride of the cow ponies. The leader remembered how the bay mare, Lou, had skimmed over the ground. She was the queen of horses, and this pair were like dirt compared with her! Yes, Jerry Dawn had struck her blow at the vital moment, and perhaps in the end she would win. With anxious eyes Jack Moon turned and scanned what lay behind.

All his sacrifice, he felt a moment later, would be in vain, for now, over the top of the mountain far behind, skimmed the form of the bay mare, Lou, running as smoothly as ever, running with exhaustless strength, and with the sunlight flashing from her wet sides. While Moon looked, the pursuer, small in the distance, tore off his hat and waved it — a cheering sign to the girl, a nameless threat to Jack Moon.

# CHAPTER XXX

# THE TRAIL ENDS

Straight west Ronicky Doone had sent Lou when he parted from Hugh Dawn. There was not a chance in ten that he would come on signs of the fugitive, if indeed the bandit had taken this way. It only remained to play the single chance bravely and strongly. So he laid a true course due west and let the mare do her gallant best. Then, when the sun was well up, and before and behind him the mountains were tossing in endless waves of rocky summits, he saw the two figures hurrying far before him over a crest two ranges away. At the very moment when the two looked back and saw him, he had sighted them, and, though at that distance he could not tell whether or not one was a man and one was a woman, he sent Lou like a red-bay streak down the mountainside.

But when he struck the opposite slope, unlike the blind eagerness of the outlaw, and even though he were groaning at the thought of a further delay, Ronicky drew down the willing mare to a slow trot. In this fashion he climbed the steep slope, even forcing Lou to come back to a steady walk when the trail rose sheer before him, and finally slipping from the saddle and trotting at the side of the beautiful creature.

She knew what this meant. When the master so favored her, to lighten her burden, it meant that he expected her, sooner or later, to give every ounce of her energy in his service. Well, let him make the call; she was prepared to answer. How different from the method of huge Jack Moon was this partnership of man and beast! As he trotted beside his struggling mare along that heartbreaking trail, Ronicky called out to her cheerily and patted her shining shoulder. When they reached the top of the heavy grade, he jumped into the saddle and was off like the wind.

Down the next mountainside they dipped and climbed the farther rise. Down they went again, and, reaching the farther summit, Ronicky stiffened in the saddle and cried out in joy.

Straight down below him lay the struggling figure of the prostrate gray, ruined forever. Farther still, in the hollow before the first rise, there was the glint of gold which had been thrown away. And over the first foothill —could he believe his eyes? — were the girl and Jack Moon, so close that he could identify the broad shoulders of the outlaw!

He took the shorter slope of the hill swiftly and broke on to the rolling surface of the foothills. Now, indeed, the mare could run, and Ronicky let her head go. He kept a rein just strong enough to steady her and keep her running straight, just firm enough to straighten her out in case of a stumble; and so they flashed over range after range of the softly molded hills and came again in sight of the fugitives.

They were riding on the last range of the hills, the girl sitting straight in the saddle with the red silk bandanna fluttering about her head. Jack Moon was flogging with his quirt and alternately spurring his own mount and the horse of the girl.

But he was lost. Even had he had the speed of the long-legged grays to help him, he could not have stood off the steady challenge of Lou. She came like the wind overtaking a ship. In five minutes she would range beside them. Now Jack Moon knew that the girl had indeed ruined his effort. The delay had been fatal.

He made up his mind instantly, it seemed. Ronicky saw him cast loose the reins of the girl's horse and draw his revolver, and a terrible premonition darted through the brain of Ronicky. Was the heartless devil going to murder the woman he could not carry away with him?

But that was not the purpose of the outlaw.

"Swear by everything that's holy," he called to Jerry Dawn, "that you'll stand by with your hoss and not try to escape. Otherwise I'll kill the roan while I go back and attend to the fool that's coming up on us!"

There was no hesitation in the mind of the girl. She had seen one poor creature pistoled by this remorseless fiend of a man, and she could not face the thing again.

"I'll promise," she said. And she added fiercely:

"But you'll never come back, Jack Moon!"

He laughed scornfully.

"The man ain't born," he declared, "that can stand me off in man-to-man fight."

"That," said the girl coldly, "is why you've run away like a whipped cur ever since you sighted Ronicky Doone. Bah!"

He blinked before her scorn, and then, through his teeth, he answered: "I play safe. I took no chances. But if you think I fear him or any man, watch me now! I'll come back riding Lou!"

She trembled at the thought, but she kept her head high and showed no sign of her fear.

"You dare not face him, Jack Moon," she said fiercely. "It's the beginning of the end. You've failed from the first, ever since Ronicky Doone crossed your path. I begin to see a hundred things. Somehow you've lied and blinded me with your lies. But now, in my heart, I know that Ronicky Doone was never untrue to my father. Jack Moon, Heaven pity you, because as sure as honesty is stronger than crime, Ronicky Doone is going to kill you here on this hill. And all your tricks won't help you!"

He looked to the side.

There came the pursuer, drawing his mare back to a long and swinging canter as he saw that the outlaw no longer fled.

Moon knew that, whatever happened, he had already lost Jerry. "Stand by," he said. "Watch Ronicky Doone go down. And before I go, I'll tell you the truth. I've made my play, and I've lost; but I'll show you how little you've won. It wasn't a bluff that I told my boys to run back there in the hollow. I told them to rush the house and shoot to kill. And that's what they done. Doone got away — to be finished by me. But your father is dead back yonder in the hollow. Otherwise, wouldn't he be there with Ronicky? He's dead, and that's the end of his story. And now I'll finish Ronicky's."

He saw her lips part and her eyes widen with horror; then he shut out the picture by whirling his horse toward the oncoming rider.

Ronicky Doone made out no detail of that conversation, of course, but its general tenor was unmistakable. There sat the girl with her head bowed, and her face covered by her hands. Here was Jack Moon cantering toward him.

He stopped Lou on the crest of the hill and slipped from the saddle. Why should he imperil her life by putting her in the way of a chance bullet, so long as the enemy were coming on to fight the battle out bravely, man to man, in fair contest? The good mare followed him a pace or two, whinnying softly as though to ask why he had left the saddle, but he checked her advance with a sharp word, and she halted obediently, lifting her head and pricking her ears in curiosity.

Half a dozen paces from her, Ronicky paused and dropped his right hand on his hip, for the approaching rider had also slipped his revolver into the holster now. Though he did not follow Ronicky's humane example and dismount, he came on with one hand raised in the time-honored fashion of those who request a truce. Ronicky raised his own left hand as signal that the truce was granted, and the outlaw halted not more than half a dozen paces away, still in the saddle.

He waited, his head high, his clear eye sparkling with alertness. Not a movement of the sweat-brightened body of the horse, not a stir of the face of the outlaw, escaped him.

That face was set with unutterable grimness, though Jack Moon was striving to relax his expression and adopt one of careless self-confidence. He so far succeeded that he was able to smile down to Ronicky.

"I see," he said, "that you're so plumb tired of living that you pretty near wore out your hoss trying to get close to me."

"I see," answered Ronicky, with a smile to match that of the big fellow, "that you're so plumb fond of life that you wore out two horses trying to get away from me."

Unquestionably, if there were an advantage in that exchange of words, it lay on the side of Ronicky Doone. Since, in a manner, this was first blow for him, Jack Moon set his teeth and strove to drive away the gloomy foreboding which flooded his mind. The words of the girl, too, rang through his memory. She had been strangely confident that her champion must win. That confidence had gleamed in her steady eyes, and the memory of that light now served to darken the vision of the outlaw. But he must rouse himself from this depression. In another moment his life would be staked upon his speed of hand, his lightning surety of eye, and he would be mated against a fighter such as he had never before in his life faced.

Accordingly, he stared straight into the eyes of Ronicky Doone. He had many a time made men cringe under the weight of his dominant will, but now the glance of Ronicky clashed against his own with equal force. This was to be no cheaply won victory!

But the youngster was smiling — no, he was sneering.

"Your nerve's going, Moon," he was saying calmly. "You'd better make your play now before it's all gone."

"Make my play now? Make my play first? I ain't sunk to that, kid!"

"You'll sink to that now," said Ronicky Doone. "Because you're wilting, Jack. The skunk in you is coming out to the surface. You're beat, and you know it. If you wait a minute more, you'll begin begging for life!"

The sweat poured out on the forehead of Jack Moon. For it was true! And he did know it. A great weakness was sweeping over him. The nervous, lean fingers of Ronicky Doone fascinated him. How could he expect to beat the speed of those fingers with his own great paws? If only the smaller man were within grip —

But he must act at once. Behind him the girl would look on. But the moment his hand moved

257

for his gun there would be a convulsive downward flick of the hand now hanging so loosely, so carelessly at the hip of Ronicky. How cool the man was! What a devil of surety was in him!

The chestnut, impatient, pranced a little and turned sidewise toward Ronicky. Then the trick came to the outlaw. The horse would be his bulwark. Mighty must be the bullet that could plow through the body of a horse and reach him. Quick as thought he flung himself down along the chestnut, whipping out his revolver as he fell, and, encircling the neck of the horse with his left hand, he leveled the revolver and fired under the throat of his mount point-blank at Ronicky Doone.

But swift though his maneuver had been, it was slow compared with the lightning gun play of Ronicky. At the first twitch of the big man's body, the gun had been conjured into those lean fingers, and as the right shoulder and chest of the outlaw surged down on the other side of the horse — after all, it was an old Indian trick — the blaze of Doone's gun beat that of the man-killer's by a split part of a second. A small interval, indeed, very small — but just long enough to send the soul of a man winging from its body.

Jack Moon, without a sound, without a groan, slipped out of the saddle and landed with heavy inertness on the ground, face down, and Ronicky Doone touched his shirt sleeve, where the bullet had flicked through the cloth.

He went to Jack Moon and gave the fallen man a cursory examination. It had been instant death.

Ronicky looked down with a sort of childlike wonder. How could one bullet have opened the way
for the passage of the vital spirit from that enormous frame, so cunningly made for strength and
endurance, so trained to feats of strength? How
could one bullet have stopped forever the mach-
inations of that crafty brain?

Ronicky went slowly to the girl.

She still sat with her face bowed in her arms,
but when he came near, still covering her eyes,
she reached out one hand toward him, fumbling
like a blind person.

"Ronicky!" she whispered.

"Yes?" he said gently.

"Dad?"

"All's well with him, thank Heaven!"

"Thank Heaven, and thanks to you. Oh,
Ronicky, what have you done for us?"

"Only helped your dad fight a ghost out of his
past," said Ronicky Doone as gently as before.
"Now that the ghost's gone, let's forget all about
it!"

**Max Brand** ™ is the best-known pen name of Frederick Faust, creator of Dr. Kildare™, Destry, and many other fictional characters popular with readers and viewers worldwide. Faust wrote for a variety of audiences in many genres. His enormous output, totaling approximately thirty million words or the equivalent of 530 ordinary books, covered nearly every field: crime, fantasy, historical romance, espionage, Westerns, science fiction, adventure, animal stories, love, war, and fashionable society, big business and big medicine. Eighty motion pictures have been based on his work along with many radio and television programs. For good measure he also published four volumes of poetry. Perhaps no other author has reached more people in more different ways.

Born in Seattle in 1892, orphaned early, Faust grew up in the rural San Joaquin Valley of California. At Berkeley he became a student rebel and one-man literary movement, contributing prodigiously to all campus publications. Denied a degree because of unconventional conduct, he embarked on a series of adventures culminating in New York City where, after a period of near starvation, he received simultaneous recognition as a serious poet and successful popular-prose writer. Later, he traveled widely, making his home in New York, then in Florence, and finally in Los Angeles.

Once the United States entered the Second World War, Faust abandoned his lucrative writing career and his work as a screenwriter to serve as a war correspondent with the infantry in Italy, despite his fifty-one years and a bad heart. He was killed during a night attack on a hilltop village held by the German army. New books based on magazine serials or unpublished manuscripts continue to appear. Alive and dead he has averaged a new one every four months for seventy-five years. In the U.S. alone nine publishers issue his work, plus many more in foreign countries. Yet, only recently have the full dimensions of this extraordinarily versatile and prolific writer come to be recognized and his stature as a protean literary figure in the 20th Century acknowledged. His popularity continues to grow throughout the world.

Wills    W                    Mel

MBk
4/03
& LF
11/03
Bk·Sr.
6/12